Doggone MYSTERIOUS

To Andrea,
another dog lover.
Nancy

Nancy Foster Ruhle

Nancy Foster Ruhle

Wasteland Press

www.wastelandpress.net
Shelbyville, KY USA

Doggone Mysterious
by Nancy Foster Ruhle

Second Printing – July 2012
ISBN: 978-1-60047-728-7
Library of Congress Control Number: 2012932559

Printed in the U.S.A.

0   1   2   3   4   5   6   7   8

"Dogs are not our whole life, but they make our lives whole."

~ Roger Caras, president emeritus of the ASPCA

CHAPTER 1

Hank Arrowby is a clumsy cook. Lucky for me. Whenever he drops, drips, or knocks some goodie onto the floor (my territory), I gobble up that tidbit in an instant.

Tonight's dinner should be especially rewarding, because Hank is cooking paella for our next door neighbors, Sarah Fetzler and her husband, Stuart. Both Hank and Sarah fancy themselves as gourmet cooks, and a friendly rivalry has set in. Hank is determined to wow her with this paella thing, though he may be in over his head. The dish requires a ton of ingredients, and Hank has been slicing, dicing, and measuring in between runs to scan the recipe in the open book. A prawn flips my way and I lunge for it.

"Damn it, Sammy! That's raw!" Hank scoops it up from under my nose. "Do you have to be right under my feet?"

I'm disappointed, but there'll be more opportunities. So far, I've managed to scarf up a thin strip of ham, a little chorizo sausage, and a couple cubes of salt pork. From previous experience, I know better than to lick up the peppercorn that bounces off the counter. Not something you want to do twice.

All this elaborate preparation reminds me of the time that Hank cooked a Chinese dinner for some female he had been dating. There were four different dishes, all requiring considerable prepping and last minute stir-frying, resulting in his spending so much time in the kitchen that the girl friend felt ignored and it was downhill from there. I didn't like her, anyway. She always nudged me away with her leg whenever I got between her and Hank.

I can't say I've cared for any of the females he has brought home. Not that there have been that many, especially since his accident. There was one sexy blonde who lived here about four months. She was the worst, a high-maintenance creature who demanded all of Hank's time. She dealt in antiques and insisted he accompany her on every trip to antique shows, leaving little time for me.

Why does he need girl friends, anyway? He has me. When Hank took me home from the animal shelter seven years ago, I was nothing but a heap of bedraggled black fur and he turned my life around. We're good for each other and we know it.

"Finally. All set to go." Hank limps to the refrigerator. "Man, am I glad I did the appetizer early on," he says to me.

As if on cue, the doorbell rings.

"C'mon in," yells Hank. From the fridge he retrieves a glass plate of cantaloupe wedges carefully wrapped in prosciutto. I lock my gaze on that plate, but his grip is secure.

"We come bearing gifts." The laughing melodious voice precedes the appearance of my most favorite person in the world, next to Hank. In dog terms, Sarah Fetzler is a golden retriever, with fluffy blonde hair and a perpetual smile. Six years ago, when Hank was injured fighting a fire, it was Sarah who took over the responsibility of my care. She gave me treats whether or not I deserved them and she knew just where to scratch me at the base of my skull. I adore her. I love her husband, Stu, almost as much. He always greets me with affection and a pat on the head.

Sarah puts her dessert contribution into the refrigerator (I think it's butterscotch pudding) and eyes the ingredients lined up on the counter. "Paella in August?"

"Prawns were on sale." Hank laughs. "Standing at the air-conditioned fish counter, I forgot I'd later be cooking them in the heat."

"I applaud your choice," says Stu. He lifts a wine bottle in salute to Hank. "Try this new pinot noir from the Santa Cruz Mountains. Should go well with paella." Stu can't cook like his wife and Hank, but Hank says the man does know his wines.

Hank leads them to the patio off the kitchen where a table has been set for dinner under the olive tree. One advantage of living in an older housing tract is that the trees are mature and provide welcome shade from the California summer. Ours is a typical ranch style house built in the fifties, rectangular in shape and modest in size. Perfect for a divorced man and his dog.

Hank makes Stu and Sarah comfortable with some cold white wine and the melon, while he returns to the kitchen for the first stage of cooking. I notice that he's frowning and I think he's worried about the outcome of this dinner. He mutters to himself as he puts the chicken, which has already received its spice rub, into the paella pan he borrowed from Sarah. The chicken has barely started browning when Hank slaps his forehead.

"Shoot! I forgot to chop the onion." He grabs the chef's knife and makes like Jacques Pepin, chopping so fast that several pieces fly off the counter. "Eat some onion, Sam," he says. "Maybe that'll persuade you to get out of my way." I'm more interested in the aroma of those sizzling chicken pieces. I can't help it; saliva drips onto the floor.

The chicken browned, Hank adds several more ingredients and abruptly stops. "Oh, hell, I forgot about the coriander." He rummages around in the cupboard, muttering under his breath. I wonder what coriander is and if I'd like it. He grabs a jar, searches at length for the measuring spoons that turn out to be right in front of him, and tosses the coriander in with the other things. He and I return to the patio where we sit only for a few minutes.

"Sorry to have to be going back and forth," he says. "Now I need to add the tomato sauce and rice."

Back to the kitchen we go, and Hank opens the can of tomato sauce. The opener slips in his hand just as the lid is almost off and sauce squirts over the front of his shirt. "Damn it," he says. He adds the sauce and rice to the pan and checks the recipe. "I've got five minutes before I add the water and prawns. Now, where did I put that saffron?"

He pulls the prawns from the refrigerator, checks the water simmering on the stove, and finally finds the saffron. He adds all to the mixture, then it's back to the patio. By now, Hank's face is flushed and the cowlick at the crown of his head is standing straight up.

"Are you sure I can't help?" Sarah looks concerned.

"No, no, I'm fine. It's just a lot of steps, you know?" He doesn't look so fine to me and I begin to worry whether he can pull this thing off. Then he blanches.

"Oh, no," he says. "I never scrubbed the clams."

By now we're wearing a path between the patio and the kitchen. Hank grabs a large bag from the refrigerator, proceeds to scrub the clams under running water, and dumps them into another pan where they heat until they open. Meanwhile, he turns the rice and adds some peas. It is now steaming hot in the room and sweat drips down Hank's face. "The hell with the pimientos," he tells me.

I take a good look at him. There is a large streak of tomato sauce on the front of his shirt, clam shell dirt on his left arm, an oil blotch on his right sleeve, and something in his hair that I'm guessing is a piece of chopped onion. Hank needs to break down and buy himself an apron.

When at last he serves the dish of paella with its succulent mounds of rice, prawns, sausage, chicken and clams, all nestled in a red sauce whose spicy aroma is to die for, and collapses into his own chair, he is rewarded with oohs and aahs from his friends. Stu pours the pinot noir and lifts his glass in toast. With a head full of prematurely gray hair and a face resembling that of a younger Sean Connery, Stu looks like an ad in Esquire.

"To one of my two favorite cooks," he says. "You outdid yourself tonight. Here's to friendship and future culinary delights, especially for me." They all laugh and clink their glasses together.

Sarah is the first to take a bite. Hank watches for her reaction.

"I may have put too much coriander in it," he says. "I misread the recipe."

Sarah's eyes grow wide and fill with tears. Her face becomes an alarming shade of red, to the point that I become afraid she will burst something. She grabs her glass of water and drinks the whole thing. Hank's face, in contrast, is now the color of clay.

"Oh-oh, what's wrong?" He spoons a small bit of the sauce into his mouth, grimaces, and gulps down his own water.

Stu, who has been watching the two of them, pushes his plate away. "I'm not even trying it. Sorry, Hank."

"I'm the one who needs to apologize," says Hank. "This is terrible." He looks like a bloodhound—his face sort of hanging and sad looking.

Stu and Sarah try to console him and suggest they go out for pizza, but Hank says there are raviolis in the freezer and he's determined to serve them something. Sarah helps bring the dishes of the dreaded paella into the kitchen, where Hank checks the recipe and looks at the spice ingredients still on the counter.

"Here's the culprit!" He shows a spice jar to Sarah. "Cayenne. I picked it up instead of the coriander. And I measured out too much of it, to boot." For a second, he and Sarah just look at each other and then they burst out laughing.

The substitute dinner is prepared relatively quickly and Hank uses his good Italian dinnerware to serve it. Not as pretty as the paella," he says, "but at least it's edible." He jokes about his faux pas, but I know that he's disappointed with himself.

For awhile they say little, concentrating on the dinner, until Hank addresses Stu. "I read about the proposed site of your theater project being put on hold. What's that all about?"

Hank never should have mentioned it, because now Stu is off and running with his favorite topic. His obsession, really. Stu teaches English and Drama at a local community college, and for years it has been his dream to establish a theater on San Jose's east side—an accessible, affordable place using local talent to bring the performing arts to a disadvantaged community.

"It's infuriating," says Stu. He pushes himself away from the table.

"Now you've done it," Sarah says to Hank.

Stu paces back and forth, intermittently throwing his arms upward. "Why?" he says. "Why is it so damned difficult to get anything of worth done in this city? Everyone says, 'Yes, yes, we need a resource like this in the community', but nobody wants to get off their fat arse and do anything about it. The City Council was all for it, but if it weren't for one councilwoman, it would still be just an idea on a sheet of paper."

I watch Stu as he rants on about the current problem. Most of the time he looks and acts like a stereotypical college professor, a tweedy-sort-of person with a quiet, thoughtful manner, but when something gets his dander up, the drama teacher in him comes to the fore.

Hank and Sarah continue their meal without comment, letting Stu's outburst run its course until finally the man shuts up and returns to the table.

"I'm sorry," he says.

By now Hank has cleaned his plate. Since there is no more chance of dropped morsels from him, I move to Sarah's side across the table where she is still engrossed in the food. Sarah is far neater in her eating habits than Hank, but I'm a dog and I never give up hope.

"Sammy, darling," says Sarah. "Are you saying the pickings are no longer good on the other side of the table?" She reaches down to scratch me just behind the ears and I squirm with pleasure.

"Don't let him pester you," says Hank. "You'd never know he already had his dinner. Come here, Sam."

"He's not pestering me," Sarah says. "You stay right here, my baby. And if something happens to jump off my plate, you just help yourself. Ignore that mean old man over there."

We all know this is a joke.

"I hear the mailbox monster has struck again," says Stu.

For the past month, mailboxes in the neighborhood have been ripped from their posts or covered in graffiti or both. Usually, it's just one or two boxes at a time and there seems to be no particular system involved. So far, our mailbox has not been hit.

"Who was it this time?" asks Hank.

"The brown shingled house at the other end of the street. Don't know their name."

Our street is in an unincorporated part of San Jose, meaning we have no sidewalks or streetlights, and our mailboxes line the edge of the street. Some homeowners, especially those who remodeled their places, got quite creative with the mailboxes, painting them with flowers or birds, setting them on unusual posts, or placing them inside miniature houses.

"Isn't that the house with the cat on the mailbox?" asks Hank.

I know the one. A fake cat lies on top of the mailbox and the first time I saw it I tried to scare it off. I was mortified to discover it wasn't real. I'm glad the thing was vandalized.

The conversation continues, but it lacks the vitality of their usual dinners together. Hank is subdued, and I know the paella disaster still rankles him. Stu appears distracted, probably thinking about his all-consuming theatre project. Even Sarah is not as animated as usual. Humans—who can figure them out? I fall asleep on my bed in the corner where I dream that all the mailboxes on our street are covered in tomato sauce and devoured by a giant clam.

CHAPTER 2

First thing in the morning, Hank and I head for the dog park. Hank uses his cane whenever outside the house, and it helps him move surprisingly fast, so we reach the dog park within ten minutes. This is my favorite activity of the week—chasing other pooches, pretend-fighting, peeing, sniffing, and generally just having a good time. There's a young Shih Tzu I have my eye on, as well, but she's not there today. Li-Li is her name. Li-Li and I enjoy each other's company, but the relationship is purely platonic because I've been neutered. Neutering is a touchy subject with me. Don't ask.

I'm so lucky that it was Hank who selected me from the motley bunch at the animal shelter. Or maybe it's that I selected him. When I first spotted him strolling down the aisle, eyeing all the dogs, I knew he was the man for me. Maybe it was the way he looked at all of us, carefully checking us out in a kind sort of way. Or the way his hair refused to lie flat where his cowlick was, which made him seem down-to-earth and approachable.

I had been having a bad day, still recovering from the neutering and the week when I had been lost on the streets, abandoned by my original owner. Now my hopes soared. My dog run was the next to the last one, in between a yappy little beagle and an elderly Irish setter who was missing an ear. When this human reached my run at last, he stopped and peered through the wire mesh at me. His eyes were the color of milk chocolate and gazed at me with such intensity that for a moment I feared I had made a mistake—that he was a veterinarian, not a guy looking for a dog.

"Hey there, fella," he said. He glanced at the name taped to the door. "Sammy. It says you're a black lab/Brittany spaniel mix and two years old. Good."

I whirled my tail around and lifted my front paws up onto the bar where I could get a good sniff of him. He smelled like soap and peanut butter and something I couldn't identify but later learned was modeling clay.

"Do I pass the test?" he asked me. His eyes wrinkled up at the edges.

I tried to talk. Of course it came out as whining gibberish, but it must have meant something to Hank, because he gave me a huge lopsided grin. He turned away and hurried down the hall. I was devastated, not realizing he first had to complete paperwork. When he returned twenty minutes later with Maisie, a volunteer worker, I barked with excitement, turning in circles like an idiot. Maisie opened the door and I flew into Hank's arms.

"Easy there, Sammy," he said.

I responded with licks all over his face and he laughed.

"Is that dog happy or what?" said Maisie.

She snapped the leash to my collar and handed it to Hank. We walked down the aisle, through the lobby, and out the front door into the California sunshine. From that moment on we were bonded forever.

After our park excursion, Hank immerses himself in his potting. The garage serves as his studio, a low bench and potter's wheel in the center, with shelves lining the walls and a kiln in the back left corner. He put in a large sink in the right corner opposite it, on the other side of the door that leads to our kitchen.

He wasn't always a potter. When we first met, he worked as a captain with the San Jose Fire Department. One year later the roof of a flaming building collapsed under him and his left leg was crushed, ending his career. It was during his year in rehab that he discovered pottery making. I've heard him tell people how surprised he was to find he had a gift for the art. A truly special gift, if you ask me.

I watch him now at his potter's bench, hunched over a blob of clay. He centers it, establishes the bottom, and once he is sure of the position, he starts the wheel spinning. With wet hands he begins to shape the piece. He is like a magician, taking a formless wet lump and transforming it into a recognizable object that later, after firing and glazing, will become a beautiful bowl or plate or vase. This one looks as if it might be a small bowl. Although he's not a big man, Hank has large agile hands, which quickly and confidently transform the clay. I like to watch him when he is so intent on his creation, curving over the clay, pursing his lips at times, oblivious to his surroundings. The spinning wheel mesmerizes me until I finally fall asleep on my rug in the corner, where I spend the rest of the afternoon.

Sunday morning is far more interesting. When we go out for the paper at eight o'clock, we discover it's wet from being thrown into a small puddle. It rained during the night, from about four o'clock to six o'clock, highly unusual for San Jose in August. Hank is so angry over the paper not having been protected by plastic that he almost misses an astonishing sight. Our mailbox is lying on the ground. The post has been splintered.

"Damn it all!" Hank jabs the post with his cane and scraps of wood fly off. Sniffing around the mailbox and then the post, I pick up all sorts of human scents, but none that I can immediately place.

"Get away from there, Sam," says Hank. "You'll get splinters up your nose."

He picks up the mailbox with the section of post still attached to it, carries it to the side yard, and heads for the Fetzler's house with me close behind. "Gotta have Stu and Sarah come out to see this," he mutters.

Hank rings the doorbell. No answer. He rings again. Stu and Sarah are early risers, so we're surprised they're not up. Just as Hank turns to leave, the door is yanked open.

Stuart stares at us, his hair disheveled, a stubble of beard shadowing his jaw, and dark blotches under his eyes. His clothes look rumpled, as if he'd slept in them.

"I'm sorry, Stu," says Hank. "I thought you'd be up." He hesitates and squints his eyes at his friend. "You look awful."

"Hank, a terrible thing has happened." Stuart's voice croaks. "Sarah is missing."

CHAPTER 3

The three of us stand there for a moment, suspended in time, as if we can't quite grasp the enormity of what Stu has just said.

"Come in, come in," Stu says, opening the door wider. "I'll explain."

Hank stumbles as we enter the foyer, barely catching himself with his cane. The darkness of the room is striped with the sunlight that pokes itself through the partly closed plantation shutters. Terra cotta tiles on the floor feel cool to my paws and I would find it soothing, except that there is an unsettling silence in the house.

We follow Stu into the large living room on the right where both men collapse into chairs. Hank stares at Stu, who sits bent forward with his elbows resting on his knees and his head hanging. I sit attentively at Hank's side, my ears pricked up so that I don't miss a word.

"What do you mean, Stu?"

Stu raises his head and there is so much pain in his blue eyes that I have to look away. His voice is small and quiet. "She vanished. Went off in her car and never came back."

"When?"

"Yesterday afternoon. I was in my den, writing up another proposal for the theater and she stopped at the door to say she was leaving and would be back later. By seven o'clock she hadn't returned, but I wasn't too worried, because sometimes she has dinner out with colleagues, and anyway, I thought maybe she'd told me where she was going and I hadn't heard her. You know how I am; I become engrossed in my work and only half hear what somebody's saying to me."

Stuart hangs his head again and slowly swings it side to side. "I waited up for her until eleven o'clock, and I was kicking myself that I didn't pay attention to what she had said. Finally I just fell asleep." He raises his head to look at Hank and his eyes glisten. "She never came home, Hank."

It may be a cliché to say the hairs on your back stand on end, but in my case it's true.

"Did she leave in her car?" asks Hank.

"Car's gone."

"Did you check the hospitals?"

"No, I just got up. Guess I'd better do that, although I would have been notified if there had been an accident, wouldn't I?"

"You should do it anyway, Stu."

While Stuart makes phone calls, I search the house. I know it's crazy, but I need to prove to myself that Sarah truly is not here. The Fetzlers remodeled a year ago and the place is quite large, so it takes me awhile to cover both floors. I start in the spotless kitchen, and in spite of the remaining odors from meals and cleaning products I detect the smell that is uniquely Sarah's. I sniff in front of the refrigerator, past the sink, along the drawers, around the island, everywhere, and from there I make my way down the hall and into her study.

Of course her scent is overpowering in this room. When Hank was hospitalized and the Fetzlers took me in, I spent many an hour here lying on a quilt, watching Sarah at her computer. At the time of the house remodel, she had a European furniture system installed in this room, making it into a streamlined, efficient office where nothing is ever out of place. Native American baskets share space on shelves with books and on one wall hangs a Navajo weaving. Sarah has often joked about being a Native American in a previous life, but I think a part of her actually believes it. I stare at the weaving now, willing the spirits held in it to lead us to Sarah.

Across the hall in Stu's study, very little of Sarah is detectable. The room is messy, a complete opposite of hers, and filled with Stu's scent. I proceed upstairs where the concentrations of human odor are predictable: Stu's scent is heavy in his bathroom, Sarah's in hers, and a combination in their bedroom. Sarah allowed her feminine side to take over when she decorated this room. The king-sized bed is covered with a puffy quilt of rose and pink and lavender in a floral design and floral prints adorn the walls. The bed is unmade, the quilt pushed to the side. I sniff under the bed skirt and poke my nose into closets. Sarah's scent is all over the place, but my foxy beautiful friend herself is not.

I return to the living room where Stu holds the portable phone and Hank sits next to him on the sofa with a telephone index. Hank shoots me a look, a what-have-you-been-up-to expression on his face, but I think he knows I've been searching.

"That's it for hospitals," says Stu. "I don't know who else I can call, unless it's Miriam Weinberg."

Miriam has been Sarah's partner in their psychotherapy practice for sixteen years and she is Sarah's best friend. I got to know her when Sarah was caring for me and would occasionally take me with her to work. Miriam is a jolly middle-aged lady with a practical mind and a loving heart. Something about her presence is reassuring and I wish she were here now.

"I know Sarah's an only child," says Hank, "but are there any cousins or other relatives in the area?"

"None. The nearest one is a cousin in Portland."

"Any possibility she went to Mendocino to check on her parents?" Sarah's mother has Alzheimer's and is cared for at home by her husband. The elderly couple retired to that quaint community north of San Francisco when Sarah's dad retired.

Stuart snorts in dismissal at Hank's question. "Of course not. She didn't leave with any suitcases. Anyway, she would have discussed that with me beforehand, plus she wouldn't have waited until late on Saturday to leave. It's a long way, remember?

"Sorry. I'm only trying to think of all the angles."

"I'm going to give Miriam Weinberg a call." Stuart punches in the number and listens for a bit. "Miriam? This is Stu. It's Sunday morning, around eight-thirty, I think. By any chance, do you know where Sarah is? I know this sounds crazy, but she didn't come home last night. Call me when you get in. Please." Stu's voice cracks a little on the last word.

He pokes a button on the phone, rests his arms on his knees, and just sits there with his head hanging down, like a dog that has been whipped.

"I suppose I'd better call the police," he says.

"The sheriff's office," says Hank. "We're County, remember? Where's your phone book?"

With Stu's direction, Hank finds the book and they manage to reach the Sheriffs Department. For two ordinarily competent guys, Hank and Stu seem to be awfully discombobulated. For that matter, so am I. It's not every day that someone you love goes missing. Stu is not on the phone for very long.

"What'd they say?" asks Hank.

Stu shakes his head. "Won't take a report unless it's a child or elderly person. Have to wait twenty-four hours. Christ!" He gets up and paces. Back and forth. Back and forth. I'm dizzy from watching him.

"Let's call Pete," says Hank. "I know he's a city cop, but maybe he'll have a suggestion, something we can do in the meantime."

Good idea, I'm thinking. Pete and Hank grew up together, and have maintained a close friendship over the years, so Pete will be willing to help. Too bad he's with the San Jose PD and not the Sheriff's Department.

Stu hands over the phone, but when Hank tries Pete's number he gets only a recording. "Shoot!" he says.

He limps to the window, staring at the houses across the street. "I'll check with the neighbors. Maybe somebody saw something."

"Like what?"

"I dunno. Something. Anything. You stay by the phone and Sammy and I'll canvass the neighborhood."

Sounds good to me. I'm at Hank's side, ready for action.

CHAPTER 4

Out on the sidewalk Hank stands motionless for a moment, staring down the street. He shakes his head, probably because he can't quite believe this is happening; I know I can't.

"C'mon, Sam," he says, tapping his cane on the sidewalk. "We'll do houses on this side first."

We pass our own house and ring the doorbell of our other next door neighbors. Both cars are in the driveway, so I figure people are home. In this neighborhood most people use their garages for purposes other than automobiles, although the Fetzlers are an exception, perhaps because they remodeled their house. Theirs is the neatest place on the block and you never see their cars parked in the driveway.

Hank rings the bell again. Still no response.

"Must not be up yet," Hank says, looking at his watch.

We try two more houses on this side and the people are home, but nobody recalls seeing Sarah yesterday. One man expresses doubt that Sarah is actually missing.

"Sarah Fetzler is a pretty independent woman," he says. "She'll no doubt show up this morning and Stuart is going to be embarrassed that he sent you out interviewing the neighbors."

Hank bristles. "He didn't send me out. I volunteered to ask if anyone had seen her or noticed anything unusual." He starts to say something else, then apparently thinks better of it, and just turns around abruptly.

The door slams behind us and Hank says, "Sheesh!"

We try the fourth house, where Brick lives, and I hang back just a little. I don't care for Brick. His real name is Arthur Foyt, but he's known as Brick to everyone, perhaps because he's built like a brick—flat and thick. A reclusive man, he lives with his mother and spends all his time making three-dimensional pictures out of scrap materials.

Mrs. Foyt answers the door in her bathrobe. She's a kindly old lady with an upturned pug nose and jowls like a bulldog.

"Good morning, Hank," she says. "Please excuse my bathrobe. I'm just getting ready for church. Do you need something?"

"Sorry," says Hank. "I'll be brief." He gives a short version of the situation, whereupon Mrs. Foyt opens the door.

"Come inside," she says. "I don't have to leave this very minute."

She leans over to pat me on the head as I squeeze by Hank. "Good boy," she says.

Most people understand that everywhere Hank goes I go. The exceptions are restaurants, markets, certain trails, and a few other places. It helps that I'm exceptionally well mannered.

As Mrs. Foyt and Hank talk, I gaze around the room. Mrs. Foyt must have a space phobia, because there is not a free surface in the place. Every side table is loaded with doilies, doodads and lamps, framed photographs crowd the mantel, and the coffee table is covered with newspapers and magazines. She has double rows of framed prints on the walls, which, because the room is wallpapered, makes me feel cross-eyed.

One three-dimensional piece draws my attention. It hangs next to a doorway and I know it must be a work of Brick's, because it makes no sense to me. Watches and pieces of driftwood are nailed to it, connected with ribbons of various size and color. Small photographs of cars stick out from behind some of the watches.

As if my concentration on his work has conjured him, Brick appears in the doorway. His face is wide and flat like his body and shows no expression upon seeing us. He wears his sandy hair in a brush cut, giving you the impression you could scrub a floor with his head.

"Hi, Brick," says Hank.

"Ma, I can't find the jam," says Brick.

"I'm sorry, dear. I used the last this morning. There's another jar in the cupboard."

Brick grunts and walks away.

His mother calls out to him, "Brick! Did you see Sarah Fetzler yesterday?"

"No!" Brick answers from the other room.

Hank says, "We'd better be going. Thanks, Mrs. Foyt."

The woman's jowls dance as she shakes her head. "This is terrible, Hank. I hope you find out where she is."

As Hank and I walk away from the Foyt house, he says, "That guy is forty-five years old and nothing but a problem for his mother. You're lucky you're a dog. All you know about is eating, sleeping, and enjoying life."

It's moments such as this when I am overwhelmed with frustration. If only I could talk. Hank tells me everything, pretending that I understand him, not realizing that, in truth, I comprehend every word, every nuance, every gesture. I have a gift, but it's a curse.

We head for the house across the street and wouldn't you know it, the younger Meissner kids, all three of them, are cavorting in the yard while the parents load their SUV with coolers, beach chairs and sand pails. Seven-year-old Tommy spots me before we've even reached the sidewalk and he makes a beeline for me.

"Tommy!" yells his dad. "Don't go in the street!"

Why couldn't he just say "stay", a much more efficient way of telling the kid what to do? Tommy, of course, pays no attention and almost knocks over Hank in his rush over to me. Dogs are better trained than kids, if you ask me.

"Hey, little buddy, take it easy," Hank says. "Never run at a dog."

Too late. Tommy is already vigorously rubbing my head and sticking his nose into mine. What the hell, I give him a slurp, discovering there's jam around his lips, which naturally requires more licking on my part. Tommy squeals and scampers off to the SUV.

The other two little monsters now run toward us, and we have yet to reach Mr. and Mrs. Meissner. It strikes me that the parents may use their offspring as guard dogs to ward off the public. I know I'd keep far away from them if it weren't for the fact that we're on an important mission.

"Hello there, Hank," calls Mr. Meissner, while I submit to petting, pounding, and tail pulling. "Out for a stroll?"

"Not exactly," says Hank.

The kids finally lose interest in me and grab beach toys lying next to the vehicle while Hank explains the Fetzler situation to Mrs. and Mrs. Meissner. Meanwhile, I explore a cooler whose lid is partly open. Do I detect hot dogs? No doubt about it. There they are, resting right near the top, directly under my nose. Under ordinary circumstances, I might have restrained myself, but these Meissner brats rob me of my patience and I can't help it. I grab the package.

"Sam! Drop it!" Hank is livid.

Aw, hell. I pull my head out of the cooler and pretend interest in a clump of grass.

"I'm sorry," Hank says to the Meissners. "He's usually better mannered."

"It's okay," says Mrs. Meissner. "Dogs will be dogs."

"Is Anthony around?" Anthony is fourteen, considerably older than his siblings. "I wonder if he saw anything."

Mr. Meissner jerks his head toward the house. "He's inside, waiting until the last minute. Anthony finds it embarrassing to be seen with his family. Teenagers, they're another breed, believe me."

"I'll check with him," says Mrs. Meissner, entering the house. She soon returns, shaking her head. "Anthony hasn't seen Sarah. This is so awful. I hope she turns up soon."

"Don't we all," says Hank, motioning for me to heel as we walk away. "What's the matter with you?" he says to me. "Swiping that food. You know better than that."

I sulk and refuse to look at him while we stop at the next two houses. Cars are gone at the first place and nobody answers the door at the second.

The next residence belongs to Bud Manolo, who swings the door wide open for us. Bud Manolo is an old guy—sixty, seventy, eighty, who knows how many years. Bud hails from Maui and he likes to wear colorful Hawaiian shirts. He doesn't like to wash them, however. In fact, Bud fails to clean most anything at his place, and some of the neighbors complain that his house is an eyesore. It should have been repainted years ago and grass is growing in spots on the tar and gravel roof. Half of Bud's teeth are missing, he garbles his words, and saliva often drools from his mouth while he talks. I love him.

"Toppa the mornin' to ya," he bellows.

"I didn't know you were Irish," says Hank.

Bud laughs.

"And how's my favorite ol' dog?" he asks, and strokes my head.

I sit at his feet and nudge his leg just to let him know I appreciate his attention. His pants smell like sardines.

Bud wants us to come in and chew the fat, but his expression turns sour when Hank tells him about Sarah.

"Sorry to hear that," says Bud. "Can't help ya, though. Not seen her for days." Saliva spews from his mouth.

We take our leave, reluctantly in my case, to head for Crabby Crawford's house, directly across from ours. Crabby's real name is Loretta, but everyone refers to her as Crabby because she is the most unfriendly person on the block. She is also the neighborhood snoop, always looking out her window or rocking on the front porch. And she hates dogs.

Unfortunately, Crabby is home. In response to the doorbell, she opens the door only as far as the security chain allows, one eye peering at us from the dark.

"What do you want?" she demands.

"Mrs. Crawford?" Hanks voice is so honeyed it would attract bees. "I'm so sorry to bother you, but I'm wondering if you saw Sarah Fetzler yesterday. She's been missing since the afternoon."

The door bangs shut so suddenly that both Hank and I jump. Just as quickly it's reopened, free from its chain.

"Why do you think she's missing?" Crabby asks, as if Hank were spouting nonsense.

I can hardly keep from staring at her. Pure white hair tops her pale face, which is centered with a beak-like nose, and her body is round and shapeless. Crabby looks like a chicken, Plymouth Rock variety. What's more, her hobby involves hen's eggs; she makes Christmas ornaments out of the empty shells, complete with miniature scenes inside. She keeps supplies in a portable toolbox and often works on her creations while sitting on her front porch. It pains me to admit that some of the ornaments are actually beautiful.

Hank maintains his cool. "Because Stu says she never came home last night."

"I saw her leave yesterday afternoon."

Crabby's voice is like a chicken's, too. Squaky. Sharp. If she ever laughed, it would doubtless be a cackle,

"Really?" Hank leans forward in eagerness, "Tell me, Mrs. Crawford, when was it? Was she alone? In her car? Did you notice anything unusual?"

Crabby appears to soften, ever so little.

"Let's sit on the porch," she says.

As she steps off the threshold she notices me for the first time. "Must that dog be here? I don't want fleas on my front porch."

Fleas? I shudder with indignation.

"Sam doesn't have fleas," says Hank.

"How can you be sure?"

"He gets a medication."

"All it takes is one flea, you know."

"He doesn't have fleas, Mrs. Crawford."

Crabby sniffs and Hank has me lie down while he and Crabby settle themselves in rocking chairs.

"Please tell me everything you remember about seeing Sarah yesterday," says Hank.

Crabby takes her time answering. She sits every day on her porch or at her window, observing all the comings and goings in the neighborhood, with nobody to share the gossip. At last she has an eager listener and it's obvious that she's relishing this opportunity. She leans forward and her beady chicken eyes sparkle.

"She backed her car out from the garage at four o'clock yesterday afternoon. Then she drove down the street right past me."

"Not around the corner onto Branham, then?"

"No."

"Was she alone?"

"Yes. There was nothing unusual."

"What was she wearing?"

"That floppy purple hat she so often wears. I couldn't see her clothes very well. Maybe she was wearing a blouse. I know she had on long sleeves."

"Did she wave or smile at you?"

"No. She never looked at me. Perhaps she didn't see me."

Like hell. Everyone knows Crabby practically lives on her front porch. More likely Sarah was ignoring Crabby's nosiness, as most of the neighbors do.

"Could you tell if she looked upset?"

"All I can tell you is that it was Sarah. I certainly couldn't tell you her mood, Hank Arrowby." Crabby is fast losing her enthusiasm as witness.

Hank stands up. "Okay, Mrs. Crawford. Thanks for the information."

"You're welcome," says Crabby, twitching her beak. "Do you have more people to check with?"

"You're the last one. The Atwoods are on vacation." The Atwoods live on the corner, directly across the street from the Fetzlers.

Crabby watches us make our way toward the front sidewalk.

"Don't let that animal near my rose bush!" she calls.

Animal? It takes enormous control not to lift my leg.

CHAPTER 5

"Let's see how Stu's doing," says Hank.

When Stu opens his door it's apparent that he has showered and shaved, but his eyes still look puffy.

"C'mon in." His voice lacks its usual timbre.

We sit in the living room and Hank recounts our neighborhood survey.

"So old Crabby is the only one who saw her?" asks Stu.

"The only one. At least we know exactly what time Sarah left."

"That's good, I guess."

"Listen, Stu, why don't you come over and we can fix a brunch. I'm starving, myself."

Stu sighs. "I'm not hungry, Hank."

"You have to eat, man. I'll do an omelet. What do you say?"

Stu sighs again and I move to his side where I nudge his hand.

"What are you telling me, Sammy? You want me to come or you just want some strokes?" Stu smiles and scratches me behind my ears.

I relish his attention, glad that I can help him, even in some small way. I like Stu, and know he must be suffering as much as I am over Sarah's disappearance.

"Sorry, Hank. I don't feel up to it at the moment." Stu slowly shakes his head. "Something terrible must have happened to her. She would never stay away like this."

"It's frustrating," says Hank, "that they won't take a missing persons report for twenty-four hours."

"It makes me feel so helpless, just sitting around waiting until we can make the disappearance official. I'll call them again at four o'clock. They said they'd send a deputy sheriff out to interview me after that." Stu looks at Hank and his eyes glisten. "Hank, would you mind sitting with me then? I could use the moral support." Stu's voice cracks on the last word.

"Of course." Hank stands up. "Listen, you need to get some rest. Sam and I'll go home now and you call whenever you're ready for us."

As we leave, Hank gives Stu a gentle slap on the shoulder. Sometimes a touch says more than words.

Shortly after four o'clock Stu calls us to go over. "Thanks for coming," he says as he opens the door.

I notice his hand is shaking and I nudge it gently. Automatically he strokes my head just between the eyes, but he does so in an absent-minded way, and I can't enjoy it.

"Who is it that's coming?" asks Hank.

"Some Sheriff's Department guy. They said the name, but I can't remember."

While they talk, I roam the house again, checking out Sarah's scent. As would be expected, it's strongest in her study, but less than yesterday. I experience a stab of fear at the thought of her scent gradually dissipating to the point where I'd never smell her again. I wonder if Stu is afraid he's lost her forever. No wonder his hands are shaking.

When I return to the living room Stu is just opening the front door.

"Mr. Fetzler? I'm Sergeant Price."

The sergeant is a woman, a little on the hefty side, with a no-nonsense face. She seems surprised that Hank is present and I think he's surprised that the beat officer is female.

"This is my close friend, Hank Arrowby," says Stu, waving a hand in Hank's direction. "We're next door neighbors. I asked him to be here to help answer questions about Sarah."

Stu doesn't introduce me and I'm a tad offended. If it had been our house, Hank would have included me. Sergeant Price pays no attention to me, but I find her fascinating; rather, it's the odor of her uniform trousers that intrigues me. This woman has visited some mighty interesting places. I can smell automobiles, dirt, meat, another dog, grease, grass, and more.

"Please sit down, Deputy," says Stu. "Can I offer you some coffee or tea?"

"No, thank you." The sergeant plops herself into a club chair, positioning her clip board on her lap, and whips out a ball point.

"Now, then," she says, clicking the pen, "your wife's full name, please." She smiles in a friendly way, but those blue eyes of hers look directly at you, daring you to give her any bull.

Stu clears his throat. "Sarah Louise Fetzler."

The sergeant prints quickly on her form as Stu provides the rest of Sarah's vital statistics.

"We'd like to have a photo, Mr. Fetzler, a recent one that shows her face clearly,"

"That's easy. Sarah had to have a new professional portrait taken last year."

As Stu leaves the room, Sergeant Price wants to know if I'm Stu's dog or Hank's.

"Mine," says Hank. "His name is Sam. Do you like dogs?"

"Depends. I've met some nasty ones in the course of my job. Especially in the mountains where there are methamphetamine labs."

"I can imagine. Well, Sammy here is a really good dog. Don't know what I'd do without him. He goes everywhere with me."

The sergeant gives me a half-hearted smile, and I inhale a little more deeply, wondering if I can smell methamphetamine on her pants.

Stu returns with Sarah's picture. "How about this?"

"Perfect." Sergeant Price smiles genuinely at the photograph. "She's a lovely looking woman. Her hair is still this blonde? No color change?"

"Sarah doesn't dye her hair."

"What's her profession that she needed this picture taken?"

"She's a family therapist and this picture was for a professional directory, I think."

Sergeant Price shifts her weight. "Now. You reported Sarah missing as of four o'clock yesterday afternoon.

"More or less. I didn't look at the clock. I was working at my desk."

"Did she leave on foot or by car?"

"She took her Toyota, a blue Camry. She has personalized plates. LVLF. It means Love Life."

"What was Sarah wearing?"

Stu frowns and rubs his chin. "I don't remember exactly. I think she had on a white shirt, long-sleeved. Oh, and she did have her purple hat. Not sure if she was wearing it or holding it. It's her favorite hat. She wears it a lot. Protects her skin, you know. And yesterday was sunny."

Hank butts in. "It's a very distinctive hat, Officer. If she had been wearing it, she would have been noticeable."

"That's good to know," says the sergeant, writing away. "Was she wearing a skirt? Pants? Carrying anything?"

"Sorry, I don't remember."

"What did she say?"

"Something about seeing me later. If she said where she was going, I don't recall." Stu smiles a trifle sheepishly. "You see, I was engrossed in my own work and really didn't pay that much attention. Sarah sometimes meets with her women friends for dinner. I feel so stupid that I can't tell you what she said."

"Not to worry, Mr. Fetzler. How could you have known it would become important?"

Sergeant Price shifts in her seat again. I think her uniform is too tight.

"Do you have children?"

"No."

"What about other relatives? Somebody she might have called or visited?"

"Sarah is an only child. Her parents live in Mendocino and they're elderly. Her father takes care of her mother, who has Alzheimer's. There's a cousin in Portland whom she talks with once in awhile, and she has an uncle and some cousins in the Midwest somewhere, but she doesn't have contact with them."

"May I have her parents' names, please? Address and phone number." The sergeant writes down Stu's information carefully, double checking the spelling and numbers. She's methodical, this lady. "Have you spoken with them, Mr. Fetzler?"

"No, I hate to worry Jack. He has enough on his plate taking care of Sarah's mother. I suppose I should notify him, though."

Sergeant Price nods and tugs at her jacket. She really should consider upping the size of her uniforms.

"It would be good if he heard the news from you first, before I give him a call," she says. "Now, what friends might know something?"

"Well, there's Miriam Weinberg, another therapist. They share a practice. I left a message on Miriam's phone. If anyone knows where Sarah is, it would be Miriam."

The sergeant prints at a furious rate. Hank seems mesmerized by the scratch, scratch, scratch of her pen across the page. Hank has terrible penmanship, himself. People are always complaining that they can't read his writing. I wonder what he's thinking as he watches the sergeant.

"Does Sarah have any physical or mental condition we should know about?"

"Just that she has asthma, but that's only in the spring when olive trees bloom."

"Has there been any change in her behavior?"

"No."

"Has she received any phone calls that she seemed nervous about?"

"Nope."

"Has she mentioned seeing any suspicious person in the area? Or any client she's having trouble with?"

"No."

Now the questions are making me nervous. I notice both Stu and Hank are frowning.

"Have you and your wife been arguing recently?"

"Arguing?" Stu appears startled by the question and so does Hank. "No. Sarah and I don't argue much. We're pretty compatible, wouldn't you agree, Hank?"

Hank nods vigorously, making his cowlick jiggle. "Very compatible."

As the interview continues, I roll onto my side and stretch my neck so that my nose is under Sergeant Price's pant leg. Just as I rise up for a better sniff, Hank jabs me on the rear with his foot. I turn my head to look at him and he's not happy. He signals me to lie beside his feet, a far less interesting place than the methamphetamine pants.

"Do you know the name of her dentist?"

Stu's eyebrows shoot up. "Why do you need that?"

"In case a body is found, it would help to have her dental record already on hand." Stu gasps and the deputy adds, "On the positive side, it would save you a lot of worry if a body was found and we could prove right away that it wasn't your wife."

"All right. That makes sense. Sarah and I have the same dentist. It's Anthony Racklett. He's on the Alameda."

Stu gets up to find the address and phone number for the deputy while Sergeant Price questions Hank about his relationship with Sarah. I'm a tad irritated with her nosiness, but Hank doesn't seem to mind.

"I'd like to speak with your neighbors," says the sergeant when Stu returns. "Perhaps somebody saw something."

Hank tells her about Mrs. Crawford and points out the house to her. "Just the sort of neighbor we like," says Sergeant Price, and she grins. As she prepares to leave, she pats Stu on the shoulder. "If it's any consolation, Mr. Fetzler, more than three quarters of the time a missing person is found. Often it's simply a case of miscommunication."

"I hope you're right," says Stu, closing the door behind her. We watch through the window as Sergeant Price heads across the street. This is going to be Crabby's lucky day.

CHAPTER 6

I think it's because the two of them feel so relieved at finally getting some official action that they decide to make dinner a barbecue at our house. When Stu arrives, Hank is anxious to know about his call to Sarah's parents.

"That was the most difficult phone call I have ever made," says Stu. "Jack was in tears and he wanted to come down, but of course he can't leave Emma. I told him it's just as well that he stays there, in case Sarah contacts him."

When Hank brings the meat to the table my salivary glands jump into fifth gear. The steak is grilled perfectly to my liking, medium rare with juices that I'm dying to lick off the plates. At dinner Stu sneaks me small pieces of steak when Hank isn't looking, so I lie close to him at the table. Afterward, when Hank opens the dishwasher, I bump into a chair in my eagerness to clean the dishes.

"Carnivore," laughs Hank.

The guys are digging into ice cream when Pete Peters arrives. His real name is Malcolm, but everyone calls him Pete. Pete's another of my favorites—a tall black San Jose cop with well developed, but hunched, shoulders that look as if they'd been lifting too many weights. He and Hank have been close friends over the years, and now Pete and his family live just three blocks away from us.

"I got your message," he says. "We just got back from a camping trip. What's this about Sarah missing?"

Hank slides some ice cream and coffee under Pete's nose while Stu fills him in. Pete has the appetite of an elephant, but now he ignores the food as he listens to Stu, his gaze intent on the man's face.

"Good that you got the Missing Persons report filed," says Pete. "Who was the beat officer who took it?"

"Sergeant Price. A woman," says Hank.

"Don't know her. Of course, I don't know a lot of the Sheriff's Department staff. Too bad you're not in our jurisdiction, Stuart, so I could keep tabs on what's happening. Still, I'll help you any way I can." He shakes his head slowly. "I'm really sorry, man. You must be worried as hell. But, believe me, most of the time the missing person shows up."

"Yeah," Stu says, "that's what the officer said." He doesn't sound too convinced.

I take a whiff of Pete's jeans. He owns a St. Bernard named Betsy who is completely out of my league. As expected, Betsy's scent is all over Pete, from crotch to hem. It's so overpowering that I have to leave the room.

Not long afterward, Pete and Hank pass by me on the way to the front door.

"How's Trish?" asks Hank.

"Good. Real good. Busy, like all of us." He grins. "And still complaining about the trains."

Pete is a model railroad buff with an entire bedroom given over to a railway system complete with multiple tracks, miniature villages, bridges and mountains. He even wears an engineer's cap while operating the complicated set of controls. His wife thinks he should spend more time with yard work and household repairs than playing with trains.

"Did you walk over?"

"Yeah. I needed the exercise."

"Like hell," laughs Hank.

Pete opens the door and turns to Hank, a dark frown on his face. "How many times do I have to say it? Lock your door. You're forever leaving it unlocked and anybody could just walk right in, like I did tonight. Home burglaries are on an increase, in case you didn't know."

"Aw, Pete, you've been a cop too long."

Pete walks out the door, mumbling something about stubbornness.

We return to the living room to find Stu with his head thrown back on the sofa, eyes closed and mouth open.

"Man," says Hank, "you sure went to sleep fast."

"Not asleep," Stu mumbles.

"You'd better go home and crash," says Hank. "Or you could sleep here, if you want to."

With a grunt, Stu hoists himself from the sofa. "Thanks, no, I'll go home and get to bed. I have a class to teach tomorrow morning."

"You're kidding. Your wife is missing and you have to teach? Can't you get a substitute?"

"This isn't grade school, Hank. We don't have substitute teachers. Besides, it will be a good distraction for me."

"At least take care of yourself, Stu. Don't overwork. And keep your chin up, old friend. Sarah's going to turn up, I'm sure." Hank gives Stu a slap on the back as he goes out the door.

After adding the ice cream dishes and mugs to the dishwasher, Hank settles down with a book, but abandons it quickly. He turns on the TV, but shuts it off before the program is over. I shove my face hard into his legs and he scratches me firmly behind the ears.

"Ah, Sammy, old pal, where did she go?"

Two hours later, as he's getting ready for bed, Hank takes a call from Stu. When he hangs up, Hank looks at me.

"Bad news, Sam. Stu heard from Miriam. She was away for the weekend and has no idea where Sarah could be. As far as she knows, Sarah has clients scheduled for tomorrow. Miriam is very upset."

Miriam is not the only one. I turn in circles on my bed getting comfortable, yet I have trouble falling asleep. When sleep comes at last I dream I'm chasing a St. Bernard through a strange neighborhood, but I never catch up to her.

Hank prefers his breakfast on the high caloric side, probably because he doesn't like to stop long for lunch once he's engrossed in his potting. Today's concoction turns out to be Belgian waffles topped with yogurt and strawberries, the whole thing drenched with pure Vermont maple syrup. I'd been hoping for steak and eggs, but apparently they'd used up all the meat last night.

Hank always feeds me first—ugly nutritious stuff that's supposed to make me think I'm eating chicken and lamb. Who're they kidding? I eat it anyway, since it's filling, but it can't hold a candle to the real McCoy.

There's no dawdling over breakfast this morning. In fact, Hank barely gives me time to lick the plate. A couple of passes over maple syrup puddles and that's it. Nuts.

"Gotta get your walk in," says Hank, which sends me bounding for the leash that he keeps draped around the kitchen doorknob. I sit properly, as he's trained me. "Good boy." Then I pick up the leash in my teeth and we're off. People seem amused that I often carry my own leash. They can't appreciate the sense of freedom it gives me. My jaw gets tired, though, so I seldom do it for the entire walk.

"Hell," says Hank, when we're out front of the house. The remains of the mailbox post stick up from the ground like some weird wooden stalagmite. "I'd forgotten about the damn mailbox. I've gotta fix that before I do anything else."

I look across the street at Crabby's house, wondering what she told Sergeant Price. Probably gave her an earful about the whole neighborhood. Probably told her I'm a nasty dog, too.

We walk quickly around two blocks, as quickly as Hank can mange with his gimpy leg, that is. Halfway through the second block we encounter Li-Li, the Shih Tzu, and her owner, Mr. Biggs. I drop my leash in expectation of some serious sniffing, but Li-Li out and out ignores me, straining at her leash to pass us by. I'm crushed.

"She's on a roll today," laughs Mr. Biggs. "No time for chit chat."

I watch their receding backs, my tail wilting. Hank leans over and gives me a hug.

"Never mind, Sammy. It's impossible to understand women. Don't take it personally."

Oh, sure. Easy for him to say. He's not in love.

As soon as we return home Hank straps together the two parts of the broken post, a makeshift repair that leaves the mailbox looking as if it's had one too many.

"The hell with it," says Hank. "I'll set a proper post later."

We head for the garage where Hank intends to start a new bowl. I curl up on my rug in the corner and for awhile I watch him. After removing the prepared clay from its plastic wrapping, he carefully centers it on the wheel and then begins the process of opening up the material. With smooth practiced motions, his hands caress the clay, fingers transforming a round ugly glob into a beautifully shaped bowl. The wheel turns round and round, and it lulls me to sleep.

The sharp ring of the telephone jolts me awake. As is often the case, Hank's hands are too gooped up with clay to allow for picking up the portable, so we are subjected to annoying rings until the answering machine inside the house records the call. Ordinarily, Hank would not interrupt his work, but he must be hoping for news about Sarah, because he covers his latest creation with plastic and cleans up his hands. I follow him into the kitchen where he plays the tape.

"Hank, it's me." Stu's voice sounds breathless. "I'm calling from school. They found Sarah's car early this morning at Lexington Dam. No sign of her. A Sergeant Fillmore called me. He's coming to the house to interview me this afternoon after my last class. I'll let you know what happens." Stu's voice chokes up. "It's hell trying to teach. All I can think about is Sarah. Talk to you later."

Hank pushes the stop button and stares at me for a minute.

"Come on, Sam. We're going to Lexington Dam."

CHAPTER 7

Few things in life can equal the joy of riding in a car, unless it's riding in a car with your head out the window, which, by the way, Hank won't let me do because it's bad for my eyes, or so he claims. He's way too protective.

Hank drives an old red Volkswagen bug badly in need of restoration. In spite of this, strangers frequently ask if he wants to sell. "No, I'm planning to restore it," is his stock answer. Oh, yeah? Pigs will fly before he gets his ass in gear to do that. He's too busy throwing pots.

I sit in back behind the passenger seat. This way I get a clear view out the front window as well as the sides. No front head rest to obstruct my vision, either.

Quickly we're onto Interstate 85 and it's but a short distance to Highway 17. We head south toward the Santa Cruz Mountains, and as we pass under the Main Street Bridge in Los Gatos I spot two women walking their dogs. Los Gatos is a great dog town. Hank takes me there on Sundays when he goes to the Farmers' Market, and I have a ball socializing with the other mutts. Not today. Today we're on a mission. What the mission is, I'm not too clear.

About a mile and a half from the bridge we take the Bear Creek Road exit and U turn back onto the highway, enabling us to exit onto Alma Bridge Road. People use the names "Lexington Dam" and "Lexington Reservoir" interchangeably. The dam is at the north end of the reservoir. The reservoir itself is about two miles long, making it an ideal practice area for rowing crews. Owners of small sailboats like it, too. The reservoir is pretty low, now that it's the dry season, and the piddling amount of rain we got in the wee hours of Sunday morning did nothing. Only the winter rains will make a difference. No sailboats on the reservoir today; in fact, there's not a soul around

"Where is everybody?" Hank says. He drives past the small parking lot to the turn-around area above the boat launch. We get out of the car and carefully walk down the slope to the water. There is no sandy beach here, just dirt bordered by bushes and eucalyptus trees. Toward the far south end of the reservoir we can see a storage building on a hill, but there is no human activity there, either. California hills are gold colored in August because the grasses have long since dried up, and the gold edging the reservoir contrasts sharply with the blue of the water. Across the highway, which borders the west side, rise the Santa Cruz Mountains, covered with green forest.

Hank stares at the water. "You don't suppose she committed suicide, do you?" He turns to look at me. "I'm losing it, Sam. I'm thinking a dog is capable of conjecturing."

Little does he know.

We return to the car, Hank having a little trouble walking uphill, and we drive back to the parking lot. He stops the car and we get out again. Since I'm not on a leash, I run around the edges of the area, sniffing frantically for a scent of Sarah. Apparently many humans were here yesterday, along with several dogs. The strongest scents, though, belong to a few males, centered chiefly at one parking space. There's a diesel smell, too. And a wild animal of some sort passed by during the night.

"What am I thinking?" Hank asks himself. "I should have known the car would be impounded. Guess I expected to find a search party or something." He gazes up the trail on St. Joseph's Hill, then walks over to the dam. The Los Gatos Creek Trail hugs the dam's side, and Hank kicks a couple rocks down its steep incline. He mutters something to himself, and motions to me.

"Come on, Sam. There's nothing to see here. We might as well go home."

It's back to pot throwing in the afternoon, meaning a long nap for me. Hank finishes his work around five o'clock. I thought he would take me for a walk, but there's a sheriff's car at Stu's, and I guess he wants to be available for his friend.

When Stu comes over an hour later, he's carrying a couple of beers. He and Hank park themselves in chairs on the patio while I stretch out next to a pot of impatiens.

"That was a weird experience." Stu takes several gulps of beer. "Now I understand how a suspect feels. They kept looking at me, asking a question and then just boring their eyes into me. Creepy. And they asked the same questions as that Price woman. I'd already given that information."

"You said 'they'. Two of them?"

"Yeah. Sergeant Fillmore and Deputy something-or-other. From Missing Persons. They were friendly enough, but the way they look at you—cripe! I'm telling you, Hank, those guys make you feel guilty for no reason."

Hank slowly rubs his chin and frowns. "I suppose the husband is always the prime suspect. You have to expect that."

"Suspect of what?" Stu's voice takes on an edgy tone. "My wife disappeared. My neighbor saw her leave. What's to suspect?"

"Don't bark at me, Stu. All I'm saying is it's natural for cops to be suspicious."

"Sorry." Stu quaffs more of his beer.

"I went up to Lexington after you called," Hank says. "I expected to find police there, maybe a search party, but the place was empty. They took the car?"

Stu nods. "Impounded it. Sergeant Fillmore told me they'll check it out thoroughly before turning it over to me. Nothing of hers was in it, they said, and there was nothing suspicious around the area."

Hank's voice is husky and he has to clear his throat. "I hate to bring this up, Stu, but what about searching the lake?"

"I asked. They don't think she went into the reservoir, because nothing was left in the car. No purse. No keys."

"That's odd. Why would she leave her car there? She would have had to hike down from the dam. It doesn't make sense."

Stu looks away and frowns, "Maybe she was meeting someone."

"Who?"

"How do I know?"

"I mean, who would she meet in some out-of-the-way spot like that?"

Stu doesn't answer, just raises his eyebrows. For a moment there is an uncomfortable silence and both men sip their beers.

"Was the car locked when they found it?" asks Hank.

"No."

"That makes even less sense. Did Sarah often leave her car unlocked?"

"The deputy asked me the same question. No, she always locked her car."

"Did they say when they thought she left it there?"

Stu shakes his head. "The only thing they could tell me was that the car was found early this morning when a deputy checked the dam and so it was probably left there yesterday. I got the impression somebody had missed his routine reservoir checks somewhere along the line. They said there'd been a crewing event yesterday and they're hoping someone might have noticed the personalized plates. Oh, and I can expect to be contacted by reporters. I never thought about that."

"That'll be good. Get the word out." There's a boyish eagerness in Hank's face as he leans forward and his eyes gleam. "We need to get some flyers made and flood the area with them. Put them up around the dam, including near the trails and at their ends. The communities in the area. Los Gatos, too."

Up to this point I've been lying quietly alongside the impatiens, listening intently, but at the change in Hank's demeanor and the prospect of some action, I approach Hank's side, my tail waving in anticipation.

"You think it's a good idea, too, don't you, Sam?" says Hank. "And Stu, we need to push those guys. Why aren't they searching the trails? Why aren't they sending divers into the reservoir? So what if there was nothing in the car. Anybody could have taken her stuff later on, since the car was unlocked."

At the sound of the doorbell, I fly through the open door to the kitchen and on to the foyer, barking all the way. Most of Hank's friends just knock and then open the door, so I know this must be somebody new.

"Sam," Hank yells, limping behind me, "knock it off."

He opens the door, revealing Miriam Weinberg, Sarah's business partner. Miriam's on the rotund side, an energetic, friendly lady who exudes confidence ordinarily, but this is no ordinary time. Tonight her forehead is wrinkled and she suddenly seems small.

Hank reaches out to her. "Miriam, I'm so glad you're here. You must be looking for Stu. Come in."

Miriam looks as if she's going to cry. "Oh, Hank, I'm so worried."

At the sound of her voice, Stu calls out her name, and Miriam hustles out to the patio where she envelops Stu in a bear hug.

"My dear," says Miriam, "you must be incredibly worried. Sarah had patients scheduled all day today, but she never showed up. Never in a million years would she be irresponsible like that."

Just as the three of them are getting resettled in chairs, Pete appears at the doorway. "Hank," he says, "What did I say about locking your door?" As he enters the patio he looks a bit sheepish at the sight of the others. "Whoops, sorry. Didn't know you had company."

"Pete," says Hank, ever the gracious host, "you know Miriam Weinberg, don't you? Sarah's partner?"

The two exchange pleasantries, then Miriam clears her throat. "Um, Stu." She frowns, tugs at her skirt and shifts her position in the chair. "I need to discuss something with you in private. About Sarah."

Stu waves his hand in the direction of Hank and Pete. "These guys are my friends, Miriam. You can talk in front of them."

"I'm not so sure," says Miriam, and her forehead wrinkles even more deeply.

Hank starts to push himself up from the chair. "Look, Pete and I'll go into the kitchen. We'll rustle up some coffee and you two can talk privately right here."

"No," says Stu. His tone is emphatic. "It's completely okay with me for you to hear what Miriam has to say." I get the impression that Stu doesn't want to be alone with Miriam.

If the furrows in Miriam's brow were any deeper, you could plant corn in them. "This is difficult to talk about," she says. "This past week I was aware that something was bothering Sarah. There never was a moment when both of us were free to sit down and talk, so I didn't ask her about it. How I regret that." Miriam looks directly at Stu. "The truth is, I'm wondering if it has anything to do with a past thing that happened."

Everyone waits expectantly, but Miriam appears to be stuck mid-stream. Finally Stu can stand it no longer. "For Pete's sake, Miriam, spit it out," he says.

"This isn't easy, Stu. I'm violating Sarah's confidence by telling you this, and it may have nothing to do with her disappearance. Then again, it might. I don't know."

Miriam massages her forehead and Hank looks like he's ready to strangle her. This lady sure can keep an audience on edge. I'm almost ready to bark at her, myself.

Taking a deep breath, Miriam exhales the word, "Okay. What you were never meant to know, Stu, is that three years ago Sarah had an affair."

It's a good thing that Stuart is sitting down, because otherwise he would have toppled right over. His jaw goes so slack I can see all his lower teeth, and his face is ashen. I glance at Hank, who doesn't look much better. Even Pete, who's not as close to Sarah, appears stunned. Dogs don't have the same attitude toward affairs as humans do, so I'm not quite so derailed. Nevertheless, I am astonished that Sarah would do such a thing.

After what feels like a year of silence, Stu croaks out the words. "Affair? Sarah? I can't believe that. An affair with whom?"

"Windsor Huddleston."

"That son-of-a-bitch!" Hank's outburst startles me so much that I feel the need to move to his side, whether to reassure myself or to hold him in check, I'm not sure.

"You know him?" Stu and Miriam utter the words simultaneously.

"Yes, I know him. That bastard." The muscles in Hank's jaw flicker back and forth and his coloring flushes. "He's a firefighter, a captain now. Not a very nice guy, I can tell you. We have a history." Hank bangs his fist on the arm of the chair. "Son-of-a-bitch!" It's a good thing Windsor Huddleston isn't in the room, because I think Hank would kill him on the spot.

Stu appears baffled. "How did she know him? And what the hell kind of name is Windsor Huddleston, anyway? Sounds like somebody in the Fortune 500."

Hank says, "He used to get ticked off when guys joked about his name, but he was okay about being called Huddleston or Hud, for short."

Miriam addresses Stu. "Sarah met him at that big festival a few years back—the one where firefighters put on a demonstration and had old fashioned relay races. He has a sideline raising indoor plants at his place in the mountains and he sells at the Farmers' Markets. That's where she met him again when we got new plants for the office." Miriam leans forward to touch Stu's arm and her face exudes kindness. "You have to understand, Stu. That was shortly after Sarah's last miscarriage. She had just turned forty, and I think the affair was nothing more than a grief reaction. A mid-life crisis, if you will. It only lasted about three months, if that. She passed it off as a meaningless fling and swore me to secrecy."

Stu slowly shakes his head, mumbling his words. "I never knew."

"Miriam," Pete interjects, "do you think Sarah's recent preoccupation and the old affair could be related?"

"I don't know," says Miriam. "I really don't know."

"It may be nothing," says Pete, "but the guys from Missing Persons should be told about this."

"Should I be the one to call?" asks Miriam.

"Yeah," says Pete, "you're the one who knows about it."

"All right." You can see that Miriam is less than thrilled at the prospect. "Hank," she says, "you mentioned that you and Windsor Huddleston have a history. What do you mean?"

"There was an incident a few years ago when we were assigned to the same station. He came on to my girlfriend, told her lies about me, and she believed him. Then, once he had her, he dumped her. So you can see why I don't like the guy. But a lot of fellows do, because Huddleston is smart and tough and fearless. And he's sharp enough that he made captain. He has a mean streak, though. I heard his first wife got a restraining order on him and his second marriage lasted only five months. Still, women seem to be attracted to him. I never could understand it. And Sarah—how could she have fallen under his spell?"

Miriam says, "Some women are attracted to tough men, especially if they look as if they've suffered. Sarah showed me his picture once, and he fit the bill. Remember, too, that she was at a particularly vulnerable point in her life. She made a bad decision. Fortunately, she realized her mistake in time so that it didn't end up wrecking her marriage. I find it hard to believe that she would have gone back to him."

"Maybe she didn't," says Pete, "but you have to look at all possibilities."

"Listen," says Hank, "you guys don't know this—her car was found this morning at Lexington Dam, abandoned."

"No shit," says Pete. He and Hank exchange a look.

"Why would she leave it there?" asks Miriam. "Do you suppose she met somebody there? Or do you think..." Her voice trailed off.

Stu, who has sat with his head hanging most of the time, comes alive again. "I told them they should search that water. They seemed to think she didn't commit suicide, but they said they'd consider sending in divers. They went over every inch of the car, apparently. They're returning it tomorrow."

Hank, ever the activist, says "I was telling Stu we should put up flyers, starting with Lexington and the trails leading off it and we should include Los Gatos. We could whip up something right now. You have a color copier, don't you, Stu? It should be easy. And I recently bought a lot of computer paper, so that wouldn't be a problem."

"Yeah, sure," says Stu. "We'll compose it at my house, then you can make the copies and maybe you could start posting them." Stu speaks in a monotone. I think he's still reeling from Miriam's news.

"Okay, let's get going." Hank picks up his cane and limps toward the door. His leg may slow him down, but his mind runs full tilt.

We all troop over to Stu's, and now that there's action, the group shows enthusiasm. While they struggle over designing the flyer, I wander around the house, still hoping to catch a scent of Sarah, but the odors are fainter than ever. I wonder what Huddleston smells like. Would his scent match Hank's description of him?

By the time the flyer is designed, it's late and I figure Hank will want to run off the copies tomorrow morning. I should have known better, because when Hank sets his mind to something he's like a dog with a bone; he's not going to put it down easily. He has a problem with the printer, but finally manages to crank out about fifty flyers. They did a good job with the design: at the top is the word MISSING, in large letters; right under that is Sarah's picture, a copy of the same photo that Stu gave to the deputy. Next are the details, including the name and number of a contact person if anybody has any information. Its midnight before we get to bed. As tired as I am, it's hard to fall asleep. I'm so looking forward to putting up those flyers tomorrow.

CHAPTER 8

Apparently, Hank has decided to start with Lexington Reservoir where the car was last seen. He drives to the parking lot and tapes a flyer to every power pole he can find while I nose around the bushes at the side. Even the trail sign gets a flyer.

Hank holds the door for me to jump in the back. "Well, Sammy, old pal," he says, "I feel better already. With luck, somebody just might recognize Sarah's picture and remember seeing something. Now, let's put up some flyers on Main Street where the trail crosses."

The trail from the dam lies between Los Gatos Creek and Highway 17. At Main Street in Los Gatos it is intersected where the Main Street Bridge crosses the highway. There is a little rise in the trail as it leads up to the street. Further along on the other side of the street it descends and continues alongside Los Gatos Creek for miles.

Hank drives us back into town and finds a parking space on Main St. not far from the bridge. "C'mon, Sam," he says, letting me out from the back seat, "we need to put on your leash if we're going to be walking around town." If nothing else, I'm well trained, and I sit obediently while he slips the choke chain over my head, but inside I'm seething. Leash laws! Maybe for a puppy or an ill-mannered dog, but certainly not for me. I have self-control, and it's mortifying to walk around with a tether hanging off my neck.

I'm thinking Hank parked where he did just so he'd have to walk past the fancy auto showroom on the way. We pause at the window, gazing, or should I say drooling, at the gleaming exotic automobiles on display. I wonder how much they cost. It would be nice to trade my spot in the sagging back seat of Hank's VW for the cushy leather support in a Bentley. Maybe some day.

The trail between Main Street and the dam is a popular one, especially on weekends. The yuppies like to run it and then socialize at the coffee place further up Main. Lots of other people bring their dogs and the sidewalk becomes a regular convention center. How I wish Hank would take me there on a weekend to join the throng, but he seems oblivious to it all.

Hank starts with flyers on the barrier posts that line the trail where it ends at Main Street. As he returns the masking tape to his pocket, we are surprised by a familiar figure approaching from the trail. That thick blocky body can belong to only one person—Brick Hoyt, our neighbor who makes collages. He is carrying a plastic bag weighted down by unseen objects, and upon seeing us he shifts the bag to his other hand. Hank and I had been so intent on putting up the flyers that we had missed Brick's ancient Chevy parked at the curb. We are between Brick and his car, so there is no way he can avoid us.

"Hi, Brick," says Hank. "I didn't know you were a hiker." Some day Hank's sarcasm will get him into trouble.

"You're in my way," says Brick.

I get a whiff of dirt, soda pop, and metallic odors I can't identify. When I shove my nose into Brick's bag, he yanks it away from me.

"Get away from my art," he says, and tromps past us toward his car.

"Come on, Sam." Hank tugs on my leash.

He retraces our steps down Main Street, taping flyers to light poles, two flyers on opposite sides of each pole. That must be so they'll be seen no matter which direction people are walking on the sidewalk.

We cross the street to a section of small shops. "Hey, this is a new one," Hank says, stopping in front of a store with a large window displaying paintings, small sculptures, and a ceramic bowl. The sign above the door and window reads LOS GATOS ART CO-OPERATIVE. A little bell tinkles when Hank opens the door.

Standing at the back of the room adjusting a painting is a small woman with curly red hair. She whirls around at the sound of the bell.

"Oh," she says, "you startled me. I wasn't expecting a customer this early."

Hank gives her his lopsided grin and asks if it's okay to bring his dog inside. I try to look intelligent and harmless.

"Sure," the lady says, revealing deep dimples when she smiles, "as long as she's on a leash."

She? Is the woman blind?

"It's a he," says Hank. "His name is Sammy."

"I like dogs," the lady says, and she comes closer to pat me on the head. She smells good, a little like a jasmine plant, and I submit to the patting, but I'm still a little ticked at being called a she.

"Actually, I'm not a customer," says Hank. "I'm wondering if you'd put one of these flyers in your window. A friend of mine is missing and we're hoping somebody will recognize her picture." Hank shows the woman a flyer.

"She's pretty." The lady reads the information about Sarah and hands the flyer back to Hank. "I'm sorry. You say she's a friend?"

"My next door neighbor, as a matter of fact. Her husband last saw her when she left the house Saturday afternoon." Hank relates more of the story and the woman shakes her head sympathetically.

"Of course you may post the flyer," she says. "Let's put it in the window right next to the door where people can't miss seeing it." She takes the tape Hank is holding and loses no time getting the flyer up.

Hank smiles broadly at her and thanks her profusely. She smiles back, flashing the dimples, and her eyes crinkle at the corners as she looks directly at Hank. A little warning bell sounds in my head. I don't like the way Hank is looking at her.

He switches his gaze to the paintings lining three of the walls, walks to the nearest one, a colorful abstract of who-knows-what, and examines the signature.

"I thought I recognized his work," he says. "This is very good. When did this gallery open, anyway?"

"Just two weeks ago. We're still settling in, actually. It's a co-op and everyone takes turns manning the store. This is only my third time doing it. I'm afraid I'm a better painter than a store clerk. The register scares me to death." She gives a little giggle, which annoys me.

Hank raises his eyebrows. "You have a painting hanging here?"

She points across the room. "The third one from the right."

The painting consists of blocks of colors that overlap each other. There are browns, yellows, greens, reds—almost every color you can think of. They are positioned in such a way that the painting looks like a landscape. Or maybe it's a whale. Who knows? As Hank swings his cane and limps over for a better view, I notice the lady looking at his leg.

"Ann Schaefer," Hank reads. "This is you?"

"Yep."

"You're an excellent artist, Ann. May I call you Ann?" Hank doesn't wait for a response. "I know a little bit about painting, and I think your composition is terrific." I think Hank is full of baloney.

"Are you an artist?" asks Ann.

"I'm a potter."

"Really. Professional?"

"I like to think so. I manage to sell quite a bit of my stuff, but it's mostly through word of mouth or at craft fairs."

"What's your name?"

"Sorry. Hank Arrowby." Hank smiles in a sheepish sort of way and offers his hand. The warning bell in my head is clanging at high decibels. Hank's a good-looking guy with an easy-going manner, characteristics that attract females. Ann Schaefer is eating it up.

"I'm afraid I don't know the local potters the way I know the painters and sculptors," says Ann. "Have you ever shown in a gallery?"

"I have a friend in Portland who owns a gallery and always wants my pieces, but that's not convenient. A couple of times I had things in two galleries in San Jose, but sales were slow and the commissions took out a chunk of the profit. I decided I could make more money just selling out of my studio."

"Where's your studio?"

"My garage. Very convenient, you have to admit. I put in a skylight, a sink and a kiln. It really works out quite well."

"I'd be interested in seeing your work." Ann flashes those dimples again and her eyes brighten. This is not a good sign. I do not need a woman complicating my life with Hank.

"Well, sure. Anytime. If you come by the studio, I could show you more than if I brought stuff in here."

"I work here on Tuesdays and Thursdays, so I'd be free tomorrow, if that's not too soon for you."

Man, this woman loses no time.

Hank beams. "Morning or afternoon?"

"Afternoon, I think." While she goes for a piece of paper to write down Hank's directions I notice that he's checking out her body. She's a small person, but there's a lot of curve both above and below her narrow waist. If I were a bigger dog, say the size of a Great Dane, I'd jump up right now and wipe off that silly little smile on Hank's face.

"My house is the second one from the corner of Branham," says Hank. "The VW will be in the driveway. Don't ring the doorbell, because I'll probably be in the studio. Go around to the side of the garage. There's a door there and I'll leave it open. Sam will let me know when you arrive, I can assure you."

Maybe. Maybe not.

"I know he will. He's such a good boy, aren't you Sammy, sweetheart?" She makes little kissy noises as she pats me and I want to upchuck. She doesn't even know me, yet she's acting like we're old pals.

Ann straightens up. "Hank, I'm really sorry about your neighbor. I hope she turns up."

"Me, too. Meanwhile, I have more flyers to put up. Do you have any suggestions of where would be good places in Los Gatos?"

Ann names some spots and we take our leave. It's none too soon for me.

After we've gone about two stores beyond the co-op, Hank says, "Well, what do you think, Sam? Isn't she a cutie?"

I ignore him and pee on a signpost.

"Is that a comment?" asks Hank.

Damn right!

At 4:00 we're finally able to relax at home, with Hank nursing a beer on the patio and me stretched out on the back lawn. After leaving the co-op, we managed to cover most of downtown Los Gatos with flyers. For the most part, shop owners were quite cooperative about letting us post flyers in their windows, which boosted Hank's morale considerably. Hank hardly drinks more than a quarter of his beer before he's antsy again, and tells me we need to report to Stu, if he's home.

When Stu opens his door, he's looking a heck of a lot better than he did last night and he laughs when he sees Hank holding his beer.

"What's the matter, Arrowby?" he says. "Reduced to bringing your own beer?"

He motions for us to follow him into the kitchen where he retrieves a beer for himself from the refrigerator, and he and Hank settle themselves at the table. Hank relates our experiences of posting flyers at Lexington and downtown Los Gatos. He gives all the details, but neglects to say a single word about Ann Schaefer. I find that interesting.

"And I have news for you," says Stu. "They returned Sarah's car today. They said they found nothing unusual. I'm going to clean it up and then get a car cover for it, so I don't have to look at it every time I'm in the garage. Too painful."

"It's good they didn't find anything," says Hank. "That means she must have left the car of her own volition, right?"

"I guess."

"If she went to the dam to meet somebody and then was abducted by that person, or even by some stranger who appeared while she was waiting, you would think that her purse would get left behind in the scuffle. Unless she went willingly with somebody she knew and took her purse with her."

"But she didn't lock the car."

"Oh, right." Hank sighs and massages his forehead. "None of this makes any sense."

"The deputies said they couldn't tell if there had been a struggle outside the car because it rained that night and so there were no footprints or disturbed gravel or anything. And the rain meant that it would be useless to bring in a dog to track a scent."

For a few minutes they sit silently, sipping their beers, until Stu heaves a sigh.

"I had a visit from a *Mercury News* reporter this morning," he says. "Pushy sort of guy. They're running an article about Sarah tomorrow. God, I hate this stuff being in the paper."

"Stu, what are you talking about? This is good. People will read about it and somebody will remember something. Hopefully."

"Maybe."

We're just about to go home when the phone rings. Stu reacts with a frown to whatever the person is saying.

"No, no, I don't want to be there," he says. "Yes, you can reach me at the college."

When he hangs up he answers the question poised on Hank's face. "That was Sergeant Fillmore. They're sending divers into Lexington tomorrow morning. I was given the option of being there, but no way do I want to watch that."

"I wonder if they would let me watch," says Hank.

I wonder if Hank's lost his mind. If they bring up Sarah's body, does he want to witness that?

"Why would you want to do that?" asks Stu.

"I don't know. Somehow it makes me feel as if I'm helping search for Sarah."

"It's a public place. They'll be in the water and you'll be on land, so I don't see why they'd object. Go for it."

"I intend to. Come on, Sam, time to go home." Hank pauses midway to the door. "Stu, have you thought about hiring a private investigator?"

"As long as the Sheriff's Department is doing its job, I don't see the need for that."

"Just a thought."

Stu gives me a scratch on the head as I pass him. I hardly pay any attention to him, because I'm thinking about tomorrow, and I don't know whether to anticipate it with excitement or dread.

The next day, Wednesday morning, Hank gets the *Mercury News* while I watch from the window. He waves the paper at Crabby's house, turning with a wry grin on his face. Crabby is not on her front porch, so Hank must think she's looking out the window and he wants her to know he's aware of her. He reads the headlines as he walks in the door, stopping short and frowning at the paper.

"Here it is," he says. "An article about Sarah." He reads quickly. "Good. There's a number at the Sheriff's Department for people to call if they have any information."

For once in my life, I wish I could read. It would be nice to know what they said about my friend. All I can recognize from the article is the photo of Sarah's smiling face.

Hank doesn't dawdle over breakfast today, and we're soon on the road to Lexington Dam. Interstate 85 is stop and go, but once we turn onto Highway 17, the commute traffic is heading in the opposite direction. At Lexington the lot is full of black SUVs with at least six divers pulling on their wet suits. Hank parks us in the upper lot, and to my annoyance he slips the choke chain over my head. I had looked forward to some serious sniffing around the dam, but Hank probably thinks it's unwise to have a dog off leash in the presence of so many Sheriff's deputies. We approach the man who appears to be in charge.

"Officer," says Hank, "I'm Hank Arrowby, a neighbor and friend of Sarah Fetzler, the woman you're looking for. Her husband didn't want to be around for the search, and I told him I'd look in on it. If that's okay with you."

"Yes, provided you stay out of our way. I'm Lieutenant Anderson, in charge of the dive." The man squints at Hank and points to another officer. "I'd like you to give your name and address, though, to the deputy standing by that vehicle "

Hank looks surprised, but says, "Sure." He does as requested, and we find a stump under the eucalyptus trees where we can park ourselves to watch the proceedings.

Three Zodiak boats, each holding two divers and a third man, fan out from the launch ramp. While one man stays in each boat, the two divers pull on their tanks and back flip over the sides. Periodically, the divers pull themselves back into the Zodiaks, the boats reposition themselves, and we realize that they're searching on a grid pattern. Every time the divers come up empty-handed, Hank mutters, "Good."

The Lieutenant directs the search from shore via radio. After an hour of this, the guys take breaks, change tanks, and go over the sides again. At first it's all quite interesting, but by noontime Hank and I have had our fill, and we're both hot and thirsty. We pass by the lieutenant on our way out.

"Had enough?" asks the officer.

"More than enough," says Hank. "I guess it's a good thing you're not finding anything, though."

"True."

"Is Lexington hard to search in?"

"Oh, hell, yes. It's a dam, remember, so there are hills and crevices and boulders under all that water. Not like a swimming pool, you know." I get the impression this guy is happy to see us leave, and the feeling on our side is mutual.

CHAPTER 9

It's a relief to be back in our cool house, where Hank refills my water dish and makes himself a turkey sandwich. At first he reaches for a beer in the refrigerator, but changes his mind and retrieves some bottled water. I wonder at his decision, until I remember that Ann Dimples What's-Her-Name is coming to look at his pottery this afternoon. Mustn't smell like a brewery, I suppose.

Hank reads the paper while he chews the sandwich. Periodically, he stares off into space and at one point he mutters, "I wonder what's happening at the dam." I lie on the floor watching him. Man, how I love this guy. He's forever trying to help somebody, always going the extra mile, and Lord knows he's been good to me. I never knew him when he was a captain with the fire department, but according to comments Stu and Pete have made, I know he was a top firefighter. With those friendly eyes and genuine grin, he's one attractive man. Plus that little cowlick on the crown of his head gives him a touch of vulnerability. Little wonder that Ann Redhead Picasso wants to see his pottery. Probably wants to see more than pots, too.

Hank breaks my reverie. "Nope. You're not getting any scraps. So forget about it."

Hey, who's waiting for scraps? I take back all the good thoughts I was having about him.

In the studio Hank opens the side door so that Miss Wonderful will be able to find him, and I settle on an old rug that protects my bones from the concrete. There's a wet earthy smell to the room. Hank changes to the work clothes he keeps in the studio, dons his plastic apron, fills a basin with water, and unwraps a fresh lump of clay. Centering it on the wheel, he dips a sponge in the water and starts the wheel spinning with the foot pedal. Guided by his talented hands, the clay rises like something alive. Tall and narrow, perhaps the beginning of a vase, it reminds me of a cobra.

The wheel once again mesmerizes me, sending me to dreamless sleep. I'm startled awake by a high voice.

"Helloooo. Hank?"

It's her. Damn.

"Come in, come in," says Hank, practically falling over a bag of clay while trying to get to the door. "Welcome to the studio. Your timing is perfect. I just set my bowl on the board to dry. Did you have trouble finding the place?"

Ann Schaefer walks hesitantly into the garage. "No, your directions were exact." She stops to scan the room. "It's nice and cool in here. My, it's a big place. You should see my little studio. It's half the size of this."

"Well, pottery does take up a lot of room. Mine, does, anyway." Hank sheds his big apron and heads for the sink. "Give me a minute to clean up and then I'll take you on the grand tour."

"There's your dog," she says. "Such a cutie. What did you say her, I mean his, name is?"

Can't she get the gender straight? There are only two choices, for crying out loud.

"Sam," says Hank. He looks at me. "Hey, Sammy, where are your manners? Can't you get up and say hello to the lady?"

I thump my tail just to show a response, but remain with my chin on the rug.

"Must be out of sorts this afternoon," says Hank.

"He's so sweet." Ann leans over to scratch me behind the ears. I refuse to acknowledge that it feels good.

"Did you ever do any potting?" asks Hank

"A little in art school. Just an introductory course. Enough to know I didn't like all that clay dust."

"I am a bit of a mess, aren't I?" laughs Hank, looking at his work clothes that are so covered in gray you can hardly recognize their original color. "Maybe we should skip the studio and concentrate on the finished pieces, instead. They are all inside the house." He opens the door into the kitchen. "Why don't you sit down here while I get out of these overalls. I try to avoid bringing clay dust into the house."

"Your wife won't mind my coming in?"

"No wife. Hey, Sammy, keep the lady company."

Hank motions me into the kitchen. What am I, a baby sitter?

Ann What's-Her-Face sits down at the table and cranes her neck, looking over the place. It's not the neatest kitchen in the world, but it shows her that Hank must like to cook, because spice bottles sit scattered about the counter and there is a pile of cookbooks on the end. Ten seconds later she's up and at the back window, checking out the patio.

"Mmmm. Pretty," she says.

I lie down in the corner and ignore her.

Hank soon joins us. "I have some of my works in the living room," he says. "Shall we start there?"

He limps ahead of us, and again I notice Ann eyeing his leg. We stop at a large plate atop the fireplace mantel. Its colors of bronze, teal and sand swirl and swoop into each other, catching the light differently when viewed from various angles, so that the whole thing seems to move. Everyone who visits our house comments on it. Ann Dimples is no exception.

"This is remarkable," she says. Her eyes glisten. I hope she's not going to be so sappy as to cry over a piece of pottery.

We move on to some bowls on tables, and then Hank ushers us into the room where he stores most of his finished works. One wall is covered with shelves where he displays bowls, vases, plates, and objects of unusual shape that are purely decorative art. Three rectangular tables hold larger pieces.

Ann stops at the first table. "My God," she whispers. "Oh, Hank, these are good. These are very good. May I touch them?"

"Of course." Hank is smiling, obviously gratified by her praise. Doesn't he recognize flattery when he sees it?

"The glaze on this platter is exquisite," gushes Miss Wonderful, lifting the object and holding it up to the light. "How did you do that?"

"Trade secret," Hank laughs.

Ann scrutinizes every piece of pottery in the whole damn place, lifting, turning, tipping each one like a nosy appraiser. I'm surprised she doesn't sniff them, too.

Hank looks embarrassed and doesn't comment while she oohs and aahs about every object he has in the room. Ordinarily he takes pride in showing his work to others, but today he acts almost shy. Because she's a professional artist herself? Because he's suddenly modest about his talent? Because he'd rather have her notice him for things other than his art? I don't want to think about that.

At long last she turns to Hank. "I hope you'll consider joining our co-op. The other members have to agree that your work qualifies, of course, but in your case that'd be just a formality. You'd have no problem selling your stuff, Hank."

"I have no problem now. Word of mouth gets me my sales."

Way to go, Hank! Who does this woman think she is, acting like you're a rank amateur?

"I'm sorry. I didn't mean it that way."

"I know." Hank smiles.

Oh, yeah? How does he know what she means?

At the end of the tour they discuss which pieces should go to the gallery, assuming acceptance by other co-op members, and which hours Hank might be able to volunteer.

"How about a cup of coffee?" Hank asks.

It was too much to hope that the lady would just take some samples of his work and go home where she belongs.

"I'm afraid I'm a tea drinker," says Ann.

"No problem. I have some tea on hand. Just bags, though, if that's okay."

"Sure," Ann smiles.

We move to the kitchen where Hank putters around boiling water and brewing coffee. Checking the box of tea bags, he names the choices and Ann selects a green tea. She's probably a health nut.

Hank brings out the china cups and saucers, a rather unnecessary gesture, if you ask me, but of course he wants to impress her. When he hands her the cup and saucer I notice his hand trembles ever so slightly. This is not good.

My spirits perk up when he lifts a bag of pastries from the freezer. "How about a Danish?" he asks.

"Nothing for me," she says, "but you go ahead."

Fortunately, Hank follows her suggestion and nukes a goodie for himself.

"Your dog is so cute," says Ann. "He follows your every move."

"Sure, where food is concerned," says Hank.

I'm insulted. But not for long, because a crumb soon heads my way.

The two of them settle into chairs opposite each other and for a moment there's an awkward silence.

"How long have you been doing pottery?" Ann asks.

"About four years. Since I went on disability. I read books and took classes and before I knew it I was throwing clay four hours a day. I love it."

"You have talent. What did you do before you became a potter?"

"I was a firefighter with San Jose."

"And that's how you hurt your leg?"

I knew sooner or later she'd get around to asking about his limp.

"Yep. We had a house fire in south San Jose and I was one of the guys on the roof. It was a routine situation, everything going according to plan, and then the roof collapsed underneath me. Broke my hip and every other bone in my left leg. That was the end of my firefighting career."

"How awful."

"Yeah, I was pretty messed up for awhile, physically and psychologically. It was Sarah who came to the rescue."

"Sarah? The woman who's missing?"

Hank nods. "She referred me to her partner, Miriam Weinberg, for therapy, and that helped a lot. I learned to accept the fact that my days of running and backpacking were over. Still have claustrophobia, though."

"Have there been any responses to the flyers you've put up?"

"Not yet. One good thing, however, is that divers are searching Lexington today. I was up there for awhile this morning." Hank describes the scene briefly.

"Let's talk about better things," he says. "Tell me about yourself—how you came to be an artist."

Ann smiles at him over her raised cup. Her eyes are a bright, piercing blue and she gazes directly into Hank's. Hank looks as if he's melting.

"I can't remember a time," she says, "when I wasn't drawing or painting. I majored in art at San Jose State and just kept on going." Ann shrugs her shoulders and sighs. "Unfortunately, I wasn't one of those with a huge talent, so I barely make a living. I do some teaching, which helps. I'm lucky in that I get to do what I truly love. And there's always time for hiking, which is another one of my passions."

I'd prefer she didn't use the word passion.

"I used to enjoy hiking, too," says Hank, "before my accident. The Bay Area is a perfect place for it. Where do you go?"

Ann rattles off the names of a bunch of trails, and Hank nods his head in recognition of several of them. I feel sorry for the guy because I know he must miss hiking the steeper hills. And I know he's thinking how great it would be to accompany Miss Dimples on the trails. On second thought, I'm not sorry at all.

Hank fiddles with his cup. "You said you barely make a living with your painting. There's no Mr. Schaefer to help support the starving artist?"

He's trying to make light of it, but of course he's dying to know if there's another man involved.

"No. And there never will be."

If dogs could laugh, I'd be roaring at the flicker of conflicting emotions on Hank's face. He's obviously relieved to know she's not married, but surprised and confused by her second statement. Maybe she's a lesbian. Oh, joy.

"There never will be?"

Ann bites her lower lip. "I'm sorry. That just sort of came out without thinking. After so many years you'd think I'd be less bitter, but I'm still not over it." She stares down into her cup, as if the memories are floating around like tea leaves. "Ten years ago I was engaged to the perfect man. Handsome, witty, bright, Stanford educated, headed for success in the financial world. All my friends told me how lucky I was. One itty bitty problem, though, which I discovered just two weeks before we were to be married— he was a pathological liar. Almost nothing he had told me about himself was true. He was not Stanford educated; in fact, he had only one year of college somewhere in Colorado. His parents, whom he said were dead, turned out to be very much alive. I could go on and on. I only found out about the lying because my sister met somebody who knew him from years back, and the truth came out. That experience killed something inside me. I was so shattered, I swore I'd never get married. For three years I didn't even date. Even now, when some guy tells me about himself, there's a part of me that stands aside and thinks maybe, maybe not." She suddenly beams a big dimpled smile at Hank. "But I believe you about your leg."

Hank smiles back. "Good," he says. Then his face darkens and he toys with his cup. "I know what you mean about being shattered by someone's deceit. It happened to me, too, though not as bad as with you. A guy I worked with, someone I'd trust with my life on the job, deliberately deceived me. I've never forgiven him for it."

"That's a shame," Ann says. "Relationships can be difficult sometimes."

I'm bored with this conversation and perk up when Ann changes the subject.

"What do you think happened to your neighbor?"

Hank looks up from massaging his cup. In a quiet voice he says, "I think she's dead."

"Wow." Miss Perky is suddenly somber. "Murdered?" She whispers the word.

I'd make fun of the fact that she is whispering when there are just the two of them in the room, but the thought of murder has made my skin crawl worse than a case of fleas.

Hank flinches. "I don't know. Maybe. Maybe suicide, but I don't think so."

"It's awful not to know, isn't it?"

"Let's talk about something else."

For awhile they discuss art, then walk through the house looking for the best piece to show to the co-op members. Ann chooses one of Hank's favorites, a vase glazed with swirling colors of bronze and green that make it look like aged copper. Since Ann needs to leave right away for an appointment, Hank agrees to wrap up the vase and bring it to the gallery tomorrow.

As we move toward the front door, Ann reaches down to pat me on the head.

"You're such a cutie," she gushes. "I don't think you like me, though."

How can she tell? Maybe it's because I'm standing rock still, not even wagging my tail.

Hank throws me a glance. "Aw, Sam's just being polite. When he gets to know you he'll be bugging the hell out of you."

What does he mean by "when he gets to know you." I have a sinking feeling in the pit of my stomach.

Hank is whistling when he returns from escorting Ann to the car. He scratches me hard behind my ears, sending waves of pleasure streaming down my back, and I shove my head hard into his knees.

"What's the matter? Feeling left out?" Hank chuckles. "What a dog you are."

I take that as a compliment and spend the rest of the afternoon dozing happily in the studio while Hank works on his creation.

I dream that Li-Li and I are off-leash in a park chasing squirrels, but when I stop to play with her she turns into an ugly snapping schnauzer. I wake up out-of-sorts, finding Hank has already cleaned up.

"Come on, Sam," he says. "Let's go see Stu."

Stu smiles when he opens the door, but the poor guy looks awful, with bags under his eyes and his jaw clenched like a bull terrier's. I swear his gray hair is turning white.

"Sergeant Fillmore just called," he says. "The divers didn't find anything at Lexington."

"Great news." Hank beams and slaps Stu on the shoulder.

They settle themselves in chairs in the living room, and as Hank begins to describe his experience at Lexington this morning, Stu cuts him short.

"There's more news," he says. "The car was seen parked in Santa Cruz late Saturday afternoon."

"What? Where?" Hank sits up straight and stiff in his chair, alert as a deer.

"On Columbia Street, which I gather is not far from the lighthouse."

"Are they sure it was Sarah's?"

"Sergeant Fillmore said the license plate was LVLF. No mistake."

"What time was it noticed?"

"Around six, I think he said."

"And nobody was seen in or near the car?"

"Nope."

"Sheesh!" Hank runs his fingers through his hair, causing his cowlick to pop up. "Why would Sarah drive to Santa Cruz and then back to Lexington Dam?"

Stu shrugs his shoulders and looks out the window.

"Unless," Hank says, "it wasn't Sarah who drove the car there."

Stu snaps his head around. "What are you saying? Mrs. Crawford saw her drive off."

"I know, Stu, but something could have happened to her after that. We don't know where she went."

"I keep trying to avoid thinking about what might have happened." Stu's voice cracks a little.

"Hey, we need to post some flyers in Santa Cruz near where the car was found. Got a map?"

As Stu heads for the den, we all jump at the sound of banging on the front door. Stu doesn't even have time to get to it before the door is thrown open, and there stands a guy I've never seen before. He's taller than Stu and thin with a full dark moustache that reaches the deep crevices in his cheeks. His eyes are smoky colored, maybe because they're on fire. Hank and Stu each take a step back. I'm no coward, but I move closer to Hank's side.

"Fuck you! Both of you!"

"And hello to you, too, Huddleston," says Hank.

"Huddleston?" Stu looks bewildered.

"Yeah, Stu." Hank's voice rasps. "The upstanding citizen who was banging your wife."

My skin is crawling. Hank never talks this way and it makes me nervous. There's venom in his voice.

Stu's body is rigid, his fists clenched at his side, and his face the color of a tomato. "You son of a bitch," he says.

Now I'm really worried, because Stu's usual mild-mannered demeanor is out the window, and I'm afraid there'll be a free-for-all.

Stu points a finger at Windsor Huddleston. "What right have you to come barging in here? You've got things backward, wouldn't you say?"

Huddleston flicks away Stu's finger and brushes right past him. "I got interviewed by two officers today," he says. "Not a pleasant experience. Not. They acted like I had something to do with your wife's disappearance. Yes, we had an affair. I admit that, but that was years ago. I only learned from the *Mercury* that she was missing. She probably ran off with some other guy."

"Shut up," says Stu. "What makes you think I put cops onto you? I didn't even know Sarah had an affair until two days ago. And I sure as hell didn't know who you were."

"Hud, look," says Hank, a little calmer now. "What difference does it make how the cops got your name? The important thing is that Sarah is missing and we need to find out what's happened to her. You ought to be concerned about her, not about your own ass."

"Yeah?" Huddleston's right eye twitches. "You're not the one who was drilled by those two guys."

"So what?" says Stu. "I got drilled, too. They have to do that."

Huddleston's eyes narrow and a sickly little smile plays on his face. "Maybe they had reason to drill you. Isn't the husband always the prime suspect?"

Hud's right leg is six inches away from me. He's wearing jeans and the fabric twitches when he talks. I'm seriously considering biting right through it.

"That's enough, asshole," says Hank. "Time you left."

"I wasn't aware this was your house, Hank."

Everyone's attention is diverted by the appearance of Miriam Weinberg at the open doorway. She is wearing her work clothes—a light blue skirt with a matching blouse that is rumpled after a day in the office. Little beads of perspiration shine at the top of her forehead. "Hi, guys," she says. "I came to pick up some flyers."

"Oh, good, it's Old Home Week," says Huddleston.

Miriam's mouth forms a perfect O. "Windsor Huddleston!" Miriam does not appear overjoyed at the sight of him.

Hank closes the door and takes Miriam by the arm. "Hud's pissed because he got interviewed by detectives today."

"I was interviewed, too," says Miriam. "I expect everyone who knows Sarah will get a turn."

Huddleston's tic is more pronounced and he stares at Miriam. "What time were you interviewed, Miriam?" he asks.

"Right after I got to the office this morning."

"Really. I was interviewed this afternoon. You didn't happen to tell them about the affair, did you?"

Miriam's answer is all over her face. You'd think a therapist would be more adept at keeping a blank expression, but I suppose she has been taken off guard.

Huddleston's eyes are smoking again. "You! You told them!"

Now Miriam is angry, and if I were a human I think I'd laugh. She's half the height of Huddleston and a lot flabbier, but she marches up to him and pokes her finger in his chest. It's like a pudgy little bulldog squaring off with a Doberman pinscher.

"So what!" she yells. "Everyone Sarah knows has to be questioned. You got your jollies when she was at a vulnerable time in her life; now you're too cowardly to admit it. You are a despicable ass!"

Hank is grinning, but Stu finally has had it. His face dark with rage, he swings his arm toward the door. "Out!" he shouts. "The lot of you! Get out!"

Hank makes a move toward Stu, then abruptly turns on his heel, snapping his fingers at me on his way to the door. Immediately I follow, eager to escape the tension in that room. Miriam and Hud retreat almost as fast, and the door shuts with a bang behind us.

CHAPTER 10

Hank whistles as he prepares breakfast, an attitude in sharp contrast to last evening when he and Miriam consoled each other over the incident. They talked for an hour before Miriam finally left, carrying flyers to post near her office. Dinner was a grumpy affair, with Hank hardly speaking a word to me. Now he's popping around the kitchen, occasionally tossing me crumbs.

The mysterious behavior change is subsequently explained when he starts packing up the living room vase: he's taking it to the co-op gallery; he's going to see Ann; he's happy. Damn.

Hank is careful about the packing, which takes a long time. I sit patiently by the studio door, fearful that he might leave me at home, since I'm sure he knows I don't like that woman. I wag my tail exuberantly and am rewarded when he lets me join the box in the VW.

At the gallery we find Ann Kissy-Face and another lady going through some papers. "Hank! You're here!" says Ann.

Of course he's here. He's not somewhere else, is he? The lady has a screw loose.

"Millie," says Ann, "this is Hank Arrowby, the potter I told you about."

Ann turns her beaming face to Hank. "Millie Loh is our director." They shake hands and the Millie person, bless her heart, notices me and asks Hank about me. She doesn't refer to me as she, either.

"Isn't Sam adorable?" says Ann.

Give me a break.

While Hank unpacks the vase and Millie exclaims over the piece, I sniff around the store. Already I've identified Ann's scent, which, I hate to admit, is pleasant—sort of a woodsy smell with just a touch of alyssum.

As I nose around the gallery I spot the Missing Person flyer taped to the front window. My heart lurches a bit, thinking of Sarah—the way she

56

scratches me under the collar and puts her nose up to mine and laughs when I lick her face. Now there is a woman who understands dogs.

On completion of my inspection of the store I find that Hank and Ann will lunch together, an impromptu picnic in the park, and on the way back Ann will drop off one of her paintings at a retirement center. Ann has a bag lunch already made, but Hank needs to stop at a deli on the way. While he's in the store Ann twists around in the front seat to look at me. She starts to say something, but I'm damned if I'm going to have a conversation with her, and with a little groan I lie down, averting my head.

"I don't think you like me, Sammy," she says.

Briefly I lift one eyebrow. She laughs, not the reaction I expected.

Once we arrive at Oak Meadow Park Hank slips the choke chain and leash on me and I settle myself beside the picnic table while he and Ann enjoy their lunches. Maybe Ann is a messy eater and there'll be some goodies for me.

"Your hair is redder in the sunlight," says Hank.

"Don't remind me."

"Why? Don't you like your hair?"

"Hank, no woman likes her hair: it's too curly; it's too straight; it's too red; it's too drab; it's too fine; it's too thick."

"I think yours is beautiful."

They go on like that, making small talk, and then my interest perks up when Ann asks Hank about his life as a firefighter.

"Were you ever scared?" she asks.

"Of course. Every time I went into a burning building. It's the pitch-blackness that gets you. Not like the movies, where you see the actors. In a real fire you can't see a damn thing. You have to feel your way through and it's disorienting."

Unable to see Hank's face from beneath the table, I'm super alert to changes in his voice tone. It rises just a bit on the last word.

"I can't imagine doing such work," says Ann.

"The upside is what keeps you going. There's the adrenalin rush, and of course you're a hero to everybody. Some guys get off on that hero worship thing."

"Did you always want to be a firefighter?"

"Pretty much. My dad was one in Sunnyvale, so it's probably in the genes. I loved it."

"It must have been awfully hard for you—getting hurt and having to give it up."

There's a pause and Hank shifts his feet. "Yeah, it was. But then, if that hadn't happened I wouldn't have gotten into potting, so it all worked out in the end."

Ann bounces around in her seat and her dumb little red curls bounce, too.

"It's my firm belief," she says, "When life gives you lemons, you make lemonade."

I want to toss my cookies.

"So how did you make lemonade," says Hank, "after your experience with the pathological liar?"

"Believe it or not, it made me a better artist. I was so depressed and so angry, I didn't want to be around people. I threw myself into my painting and all the emotions seemed to explode onto the canvases. Before that I think I was pretty good technically, but my paintings lacked feeling. You understand?

"Absolutely. I did sort of the same thing when I got divorced. I was still a firefighter then and I worked out my feelings on the job. By being the best firefighter I could be, I mean."

"Were you married a long time?"

Personally, I think humans should carry mini-bios on small cards in their wallets. It would eliminate these "ferreting-out-your-history" conversations. Dogs are way more efficient. One whiff of a rear end and you know all there is to know.

"Ten years," Hank says. "I married my high school sweetheart. Doesn't seem possible that was almost twenty years ago. Beth, her name was. She was a beautiful girl with all kinds of talent—writing, dancing, acting—you name it, she could do it. Trouble was, she carried emotional baggage I didn't know about until later. Her father, who I'd always thought was a nice guy, had abused her terribly as a child. She drank a lot, but because she seemed to hold her liquor so well, I didn't have sense enough to realize this was a bad sign. Four years into our marriage, she had become an alcoholic. Many times she tried recovery, but always would slide back. I stuck it out for several years; finally I gave up and got a divorce." Hank fiddles with the deli wrapping from his sandwich. "A couple of years ago I learned she had died. Killed herself with a drug overdose."

"Oh, Hank, I'm so sorry." Miss Wonderful's eyes are glistening and she lays a hand on one of his.

Hank shrugs his shoulder. He lays his other hand on top of hers, like a sandwich. I can't help myself; I bark. They both tear their eyes from each other and the hands separate.

"What's your problem?" Hank scowls at me. "Are you jealous?"

Mortified, I look away.

The two of them pack up and we drive to the retirement center on Blossom Hill Road.

"Why don't you and Sammy come in, too?" says Ann. "You can see what the place is like. I just have to give the painting to the woman who is in charge of the assisted living area."

Inside the building Ann leads us to the elevator. Hank stops abruptly, his face ashen.

"I can't," he croaks. "I can't go on the elevator. I have claustrophobia, remember?"

Ann gives him a curious look. "I'm sorry," she says. "Well, you can use the stairs, and I'll meet you. It's just one floor above."

Hanks face is flushing. "It's because of my injury in the fire. Ever since, I haven't been able to use an elevator or a port-a-potty or any place that's closed in. It's embarrassing."

"That's perfectly understandable." The red curls are bouncing with her words.

"You go up," says Hank, and tugs at my leash. "Sam and I will wait in the car."

In the VW I think about what it must be like to have claustrophobia. I hadn't known Hank had this problem, but it explains why he once wouldn't accept Pete's offer to check out the new camping tent that Pete had set up in his back yard. It must be horrible to feel that everything is closing in on you and you can't breathe. I suppose it must have been like that when Hank fell through the burning roof and lay on the floor in total darkness. I imagine being blind, in pain, and totally disoriented. I start panting.

"What's the matter, Sam?" asks Hank. "Are you too hot there in the back seat?"

On the ride back to the gallery Ann asks about the search for Sarah.

"There's something new," Hank says. "I forgot to tell you. Her car was spotted Saturday evening, the day she disappeared, parked on Columbia Street in Santa Cruz. Some person noticed the vanity plate. I'm planning to put up flyers there this afternoon."

Really? I hope he doesn't hold my barking against me and I can go along.

"What do you think, Hank?" says Ann. "Could Sarah have been running from her husband? Maybe she wanted it to look as if she had drowned in Lexington Dam."

Hank shakes his head. "No way. No way at all. Sarah and Stu have a strong marriage. I've lived next door to them for years; I should know."

"It's just a thought."

"I know. If only Stu could remember exactly what she said when she left, maybe we'd have a better idea of her intentions. As it is, none of this makes any sense,"

Hank drops Ann off and they agree on a movie date the following week. Shoot! They'll be together without me. Not good.

I love the drive over the mountains to Santa Cruz. Lucky for me, I don't get car sick, because the highway is pretty curvy. Sometimes traffic slows due to a truck in the right hand lane, but it's just temporary. The VW bug handles the curves well, although she slows on some of the steepest parts when we're trying to pass. I check out the section where they've installed a retaining wall made to resemble rock. It keeps the hill from sliding onto the highway, something that happened in the Loma Prieta earthquake. In the turnouts I notice people sitting in their cars. Overheated engines, probably. We're in the middle of a heat wave, something that doesn't bother me, but causes the humans to swelter and complain.

I look out the back window at the car behind us, a gray late-model Volvo. The driver is a neat-looking lady who must like dogs because she gives me a big smile. Just as she's passing us, a red Corvette in front decides to pass, no signal, and cuts her off. She blasts her horn and proceeds to chase him up the mountain.

"That Volvo's asking for trouble," says Hank. "He's going to end up killing himself and maybe some other people. What an ass he is."

Not he—she. And she's a sweet-faced, friendly-looking lady. How did she become a raging fool?

In the large clearing at the summit the CHP has stopped the red Corvette, but the Volvo is nowhere to be seen. The summit means we're halfway to Santa Cruz, where Hank has taken me walking by the ocean, and I hope that Columbia Street is by the water.

Santa Cruz—a city, according to Hank, that still maintains its hippy-ish independent spirit in spite of its growth. It's a college town now, but it remains a magnet for surfers. I wish Hank would move here, because I love the ocean and I'm in paradise when he throws a stick into the surf and I fetch it. Cold water, though,

We take the exit to Route 1 and turn off onto Bay Street, then West Cliff Drive. The sight of water sets me panting in anticipation and I'm pleased that the fog, so common on summer mornings, has dissipated. We round the corner past the lighthouse, turning onto Columbia Street just after Lighthouse Field State Beach. Hank parks in the shade of a tree near a neatly landscaped apartment building. It's a quiet residential neighborhood, with only an occasional car driving by, but I suppose it was a lot busier on the Saturday that Sarah disappeared. We sit there for a few minutes, Hank apparently lost in thought, and me wondering why Sarah came here, or was someone driving her?

"Nuts," says Hank, peering up and down the street. "I should have found out exactly where her car was parked. Maybe it doesn't matter. We'll just cover the whole area with flyers."

He grabs his backpack and lets me out of the car without snapping on my leash. Hank knows I'll stick by him and not go chasing after some acorn-brained squirrel.

Taping flyers to telephone poles, Hank walks up and down the street while I sniff the poles and bushes, hoping for a scent of Sarah. It's a long shot, given the time interval, but you never know.

From Columbia we cover adjacent streets; then Hank decides to walk to the Point, since it's nearby and lots of folks congregate there to watch the surfers. The tiny lighthouse is just a surfing museum now, surrounded by a small grassy area, parking lot, and a fenced sidewalk hugging the edge of the cliff. Waves roar and crash onto the cliffs near the lighthouse with a boom, shooting water high into the air and receding with a crackling noise over the rocks. According to Hank, you used to be able to walk from the lighthouse out to the point along a narrow shelf, but storms in the eighties tore away at the shore, and now the shelf is barricaded. The sea lions, lolling and barking on rocks beyond the point, can be seen only from a distance. Sure are noisy buggers.

I'm disappointed when Hank clips on the leash, but it's a rule in this public place. We walk to the edge of the sidewalk and peer over the fence. The surf is high today and even though it's Thursday a large number of guys in black wetsuits are chasing the waves. I'd like to try my hand at that— balance on a board and ride the crest of a wave all the way in to the beach.

A sexy black standard poodle sits demurely beside a lady in a red sunhat who's hypnotized by the surfers. A standard poodle is a little large for my taste, but this one commands attention. Beautifully coiffed, she holds her head proudly, ignoring my interest. I don't care how snobbish she may be, I'll let her know I'm not intimidated. I head for her seated rump when Hank jerks the leash.

"No," he says, and reels me in like a fish.

"That's okay," says the lady in the hat. "Mimi is friendly."

She thought I was afraid of her dog? The lady, I can see, now that she's facing Hank, is a stunner. A few inky black curls peek out from the hat. Her skin is a creamy pink and her light blue eyes laser through you. She also has that look I've seen on women before—predatory. A panther disguised as a woman.

Mimi stands, dwarfing me. In spite of her wagging tail, I'm less interested and I pay closer attention to what's transpiring between Mimi's owner and Hank.

"You have such a sweet dog," she says. I'm beginning to think this is a standard line women use as a come-on to men.

"What mix is he?" At least she has the sense to know I'm a male and not a purebred.

"Black lab and Brittany spaniel," says Hank, smiling.

"I'll bet he likes the water," Mimi-mom says. "Do you take him on the beach?"

She leans down to pat me and I swear she uses the gesture as a means to get closer to Hank. Some people have no sense of personal space. I can see the lady is carrying heavy ballast in the front and she doesn't seem to care that Hank is able to look right down her cleavage when she bends over.

"Do you live in Santa Cruz?" she asks, straightening up.

Hank says no and explains what he's doing here. I think he's having a hard time keeping his eyes on her face.

Mimi-mom looks shocked by Hank's story and she puts her long red fingernails on his arm.

"I'd be happy to put up some flyers for you," she says. "Give me some and I'll post them at the yacht harbor where I work."

Hank thanks her and pulls a dozen flyers from his backpack. Before we all part company they discuss various options where flyers might yield results. Hank and I spend the next twenty minutes taping flyers to light poles and the sides of trash bins, even handing out some to the few people we meet; then we make our trek back over the mountain to San Jose. I must admit the Mimi-mom surprised me. I had her figured for a floozy, but she turned out to be a helpful lady.

CHAPTER 11

Coming down Branham Lane after leaving the Interstate, Hank abruptly stops the car.

"Will you look at that," he says. "What is Brick Foyt doing?"

It's Brick, all right, and he's peering into Stu's back yard through a hole in the fence. For awhile we watch him as he walks up and down along the fence, apparently looking for more gaps. After a few minutes of that he stops, scratches himself under the left armpit, walks back to Cowper Street, and turns the corner. Hank resumes driving, and when he turns into our driveway we can see that Brick is entering his own home. Hank sits for a minute, drumming his fingers on the steering wheel, deep furrows in his forehead.

Crabby, naturally, is watching all this from her porch. After getting me out of the car, Hank crosses the street to her house with me following close behind.

"That dog should be on a leash," Crabby says.

"He'll mind his manners," says Hank.

"He should be on a leash," Crabby repeats.

Hank must want to keep Crabby on his good side, because he snaps the leash on me.

"I was wondering," says Hank, "did you happen to notice Brick a minute ago?"

"Of course." Crabby gives a little sniff of her chicken nose. "There's something wrong with that man. Fifteen minutes ago he walked to the corner, looking around as if he was afraid someone would see him. I was inside the house at the time, but I watched him from the window. Once he got down Branham a little ways he walked onto the Fetzler property, close to the fence. I came out to the porch to try to get a better look, but I couldn't see what he was doing. Then he walked back down Cowper. And then you drove into your driveway. He was acting very strange. Furtive, you might say."

"You said fifteen minutes ago? He spent all that time on the Branham side of the Fetzler's?"

"Absolutely. I checked my watch."

This woman should work for the FBI. Maybe she does.

Crabby narrows her eyes and purses her lips. "What are you thinking, Hank? Do you suppose he has something to do with Sarah's disappearance?"

I'm wondering the same thing, but Hank acts as if he hasn't heard Crabby's question.

"When you say furtive, Mrs. Crawford, precisely what do you mean?"

Crabby exaggerates a sigh and answers as if she's explaining to a child. "He kept looking around, as if he thought he was being watched. And his shoulders were hunched. Sort of sneaky, if you know what I mean."

"I see. Was he carrying anything either going or coming from the Fetzler's?"

"Not a thing."

"You're sure?"

"Of course I'm sure." Crabby lifts her chin and gives her chicken wattles a little shake. "I am very observant."

Hank covers his mouth and runs thumb and forefinger along the sides of his face. It's the sort of gesture one would make while concentrating on something, but I know Hank is doing it to hide the smile on his face.

"Anything else you saw?"

"Nothing different from his usual odd self. His mother should have had him institutionalized long ago, if you ask me."

"I don't think Brick is quite that bad. Odd, as you say, but not unable to take care of himself."

Crabby is back to shaking wattles. "I don't agree. Once his mother is gone we'll see just how capable he is of taking care of himself and that house."

Hank gives a noncommittal "mmm" and I start sniffing one of Crabby's planters where I'm sure she has used organic fertilizer. Blood meal, I'll betcha.

"What is that dog doing?" Crabby's voice is so loud it startles me, causing me to rap my head on a porch railing. Hank gives me a jerk on the leash, too, which doesn't help. It's a good thing that woman never had children, because she'd no doubt have them tied to chairs all day long just to keep them from touching anything in the house.

"You'd better take him home, Hank. I don't want him near my plants."

"Come on, Sam," Hank says. "Thanks for the information, Mrs. Crawford."

"And keep him away from that rose bush!" she calls as we near the street. She always has to have the last word.

Not surprisingly, we head to Stu's after a quick dinner. I'm sure Hank is eager to let Stu know about Brick. You'd think he would just use the phone, but years ago Hank and the Fetzlers got into the habit of popping in and out of each other's houses whenever they needed to chat.

Stu looks tired when he opens the door—deep lines in his face and a tightness around his mouth. Sort of like a turtle. I'm thinking he's aging right before our eyes. How does anyone cope when a spouse is missing? It's the not knowing what happened that must be the worst.

"I apologize, Hank," he says.

"For what?"

"Last night. Sorry I lost it, but Winston Huddleston put me over the edge. Lord, I hate him."

"He's not my favorite, either," says Hank. "And no need to apologize. Considering what you've been going through, I'm surprised you don't blow up more often."

"Yeah, well." Stu shrugs his shoulders. "Want a beer?"

"Sure." I've never heard Hank refuse a beer.

While Stu pops the beers Hank tells him about spotting Brick looking through the fence. Stu's face darkens and he paused midway in handing a bottle to Hank. "What the hell was he looking for?"

"Beats me. Crabby, of course, witnessed his coming and going."

"Leave it to her." Stu grins.

"Sam and I made a trip to Santa Cruz this afternoon," says Hank. "We scouted the street where Sarah's car was sighted and posted flyers in the area. Around the Point, too, and the lighthouse. Met a woman who works at the Yacht harbor and she even took some to post there. I need some more flyers, by the way."

In normal times Hank would have elaborated on the lady in the red hat, making it into a bigger, funnier story, but these are not normal times.

"I have some in the den," says Stu, and we follow him into that room. It's the stereotypical professor's study: books—thick and thin, large and small, paperback and hardcover—lie everywhere. They sit properly on floor-to-ceiling bookshelves, stack themselves like miniature towers on the floor, and sprawl open atop the desk. There is a filing cabinet in a corner, but it must be full, because Stu apparently uses grocery bags to file papers. Assorted items give a clue to his theatrical interest: Broadway posters, autographed photographs of some famous stage actors, and loads of books about acting.

What intrigues me most is a model of a stage on a marble-topped table in the far corner. I walk over for a closer inspection and sniff around it. It smells musty.

"Sam! Get away from that!" Hank's voice is sharp.

"That's okay," says Stu. "He can't hurt it. It's old and no doubt smells odd to him."

"What is it, anyway?" asks Hank, peering closely at it. "Looks like a weird set from some play."

"That's it, exactly." Stu laughs. "It was an assignment from a theater arts class when I was a student. We were given pieces of balsa wood and told to design a set for *Death of a Salesman*. No furniture or props, just a simple set. Supposed to get us thinking about angles, proportion, levels—how to be creative with a basic design." Stu chuckles. "One minor mistake: I only provided one doorway. See? Here at the rear. My actors would have been running into each other exiting and entering the stage. Crazy mistake."

"So why do you display it?"

"I don't know. I guess it keeps me humble."

He sweeps debris from a chair and motions to Hank to sit down. Settling into his own worn leather desk chair and pulling flyers out from a pile on top of the desk, he says, "I've had more news today."

"Good, I hope," says Hank.

"I don't know whether it's good or bad." Stu takes a long pull on his beer. "I received a call from Sergeant Fillmore. It seems the car was sighted later in the evening headed up Highway 1. The witness remembered the car because of the plates. He thinks a man was driving, but he can't be sure because it was too dark. And he couldn't see if there was a woman with him." Stu pauses for more beer.

"Where exactly on Highway 1?" asks Hank.

"I can't remember where he said. Davenport, I think. Yeah, that was it. The witness turned off Route One at that point."

"How the hell did the car end up at Lexington? The driver, whether it was Sarah or somebody else, either made a U-turn back to Santa Cruz and returned on Highway 17, or else he went inland, maybe at Half Moon Bay and then over the mountain back to Lexington, probably down Skyline. But why leave the car at Lexington?"

"I've wondered about that, too. It doesn't make any sense to me. Unless it was Sarah and she was rendezvousing with someone at the dam. If she was meeting someone a lot later than when she left the house, she might have killed time driving around Santa Cruz."

"Maybe." There is a long silence, the two men in their own worlds of thought.

"I think I should put up more flyers in Santa Cruz," Hank says. "Obviously, the car was in that area for several hours, so there must be more people who noticed it."

"Good idea. I'm sorry I haven't helped more with this, Hank. Just the few classes I'm teaching this summer seem to exhaust me and I'm not sleeping well at night. I really appreciate what the rest of you are doing. I just wish the detectives had received more calls than they have. Maybe I can help you with flyers on Saturday."

We're startled by the sharp ring of Stu's desk phone. Stu waits for the answering machine to pick up and we listen to the nasally male voice. "Mr. Fetzler? It's Dan O'Keefe at the *Mercury News*. I have a couple of questions to ask you, and I'd appreciate it if you'd give me a call." The guy leaves his number and the machine clicks off.

"Screening your calls, I see," says Hank.

"Have to." Stu runs his hand through his thick gray hair. "People are bugging me, people I barely know." Stu assumes a falsetto voice. "'Oh, Stu, this is so terrible. Are you organizing a search party?' Or it's 'Oh, Stu, I can't believe it. Maybe Sarah hit her head and has amnesia.' You can't imagine the imbecilic things some people say. And as for Dan O'Keefe—that guy didn't even have all his facts straight in his article."

"I noticed that," says Hank.

The phone rings and once again Stu waits for the machine to pick up. This time the disembodied voice is female—throaty and melodious. "It's me. I..." Stu has the receiver in his hand quicker than a cat pouncing on a mouse.

"Vera." Stu smiles and raises his eyebrows at Hank. "I'm screening my calls, as you can see. My neighbor, Hank Arrowby, is here, but I can talk for a minute. What can I do for you?"

I'm wondering why Stu didn't mention me. Maybe the Vera person doesn't care for dogs. After a short period of listening, Stu tells her he'll call her back and he hangs up.

"That was Vera Escobar," he says. "You know—the city councilwoman. We've gotten to know each other quite well since she's become my advocate for the new theater. We meet at least once a week and she's very concerned about Sarah's disappearance. Vera tends to take on other people's problems too much. I find myself trying to reassure her as much as she tries to reassure me."

"This project is really important to you, isn't it?" says Hank.

Stu stares down at his hands folded in front of him. "It's my life, Hank. I've never wanted anything so badly as I want this project to succeed." He looks up at Hank and smiles. "It's been my dream for years, you know—to bring live theatre to the average Joe who'd appreciate it but can't afford it. I'm hoping to be the artistic director." He shrugs his shoulders. "Naturally, with the city involved, there would have to be interviews and no guarantee I'd be appointed, but I'd have an advantage. Vera, you see, would go to bat for me."

Hank looks genuinely perplexed. "But, Stu, how can you be involved with this right now? I mean, with Sarah missing and all."

A shadow passes over Stu's handsome face, like a cloud crossing the moon. He looks away, and in the stillness of the room Hank's words seem to reverberate.

I'm so uncomfortable in the moment that I get up and stretch. This apparently breaks the mood, because Stu swivels his chair back to face Hank and his voice is stronger.

"It helps. As long as I'm working I don't have time to think. And thinking is something I'd prefer not to do right now. Can you understand that?"

Hank doesn't answer right away. Finally, he says, "Sure. Sure, I understand."

Stu slams both hands on his desk and gets up. "Well!" he says. "I need to eat some dinner." He hands Hank a stack of flyers. "Saturday, then?"

"You bet."

As we leave, Stu at last acknowledges me with a stroke on the head. "You're a good dog, Sammy," he says.

CHAPTER 12

The days have blurred together for the three weeks since Hank got more flyers from Stu. Dog days, Hank calls them. I don't understand what that means, because surely no dog would ask for such sweltering days. It has been so hot that Hank has often left me at home in the cool house and I haven't even cared that he's gone without me.

Yesterday marked the first break in the heat wave—just in time, too, because Ann Schaefer is coming for Sunday dinner tonight. You'd think it was Queen Elizabeth, the way Hank is running around dusting, vacuuming, scrubbing the bathroom. He mutters something about needing a mortar and pestle, and we rush over to Stu's. Sarah and Hank always used to borrow special cooking items from each other.

"Stu," Hank says, "could I borrow the mortar and pestle?"

Stu stares at him, blank-faced. "The what?"

"You know, Sarah's mortar and pestle. The thing you grind stuff with. I'm making a spice rub for the steak tonight."

Steak? Really? I drop some saliva on Stu's floor and hope he doesn't notice.

"Is that the little marble bowl with the whoozie in it?" asks Stu.

"Yeah. She usually keeps it on the counter under the spice cupboard."

"I haven't seen it there for a long time. I think she moved it. Let me look."

Stu opens drawers and pokes around in all the cupboards. "It should be here somewhere," he says, scattering equipment throughout a large drawer.

"Never mind, Stu. It's not that important."

"Sorry. You must be cooking up a gastronomic delight for Ann tonight. Getting serious are we?"

To my surprise and, I might add, to my dismay, Hank blushes. Stu grins and starts to say something, but he's interrupted by the doorbell.

"I hope it's not that damn reporter," says Stu. "Help me get rid of him if it is, would you?"

We follow him to the front door, but it is not the reporter who stands on the other side. Two serious-looking men in dark pants and sport coats face him and flash their I.D.s. The taller one, a gray-haired guy with a bristly moustache, speaks first.

"Mr. Fetzler? Sheriff's Department. May we come in?"

Stu opens the door wide and the two officers enter, eying Hank.

"I'm Detective Holcomb," says the older man, "and this is Detective Schwartz." He motions toward the muscular, swarthy young man at his side. The men shake hands and Stu introduces Hank as his close friend and neighbor.

"I guess I'll be going," says Hank.

Stu grabs him by the arm. "No, no, you stay. Why don't we all sit down?" he says and leads the men into the living room.

As they settle into the chairs, Detective Holcomb places a small tape recorder on the coffee table.

"It's standard policy for us to tape all conversations, regardless," he says. "Do you have any objection?"

Stu looks at Hank and Hank shrugs his shoulders. "I guess not," Stu murmurs, but he looks dubious.

Holcomb presses a button on the recorder and looks at Stu. "I'm sorry to say we have some bad news. A body has been found in the mountains, off Skyline, and we believe it is your wife, Sarah."

Stu's body is as rigid as stone and his face the color of plaster. He stares at the detectives, motionless except for his chest, which is moving in and out rapidly. I wonder if a man can faint. Hank reaches over and lays a hand on Stu's shoulder.

"I'm sorry, Mr. Fetzler," says Detective Holcomb. "I know this is a great shock."

"Maybe it's not her," says Stu, his words barely audible. "How can you be sure?"

"The dental records appear to be a match. I have to tell you that the body is badly decomposed and animals have gotten at the remains. The coroner has possession right now." He goes on to explain the process in the coroner's office and how Stu can make contact, but Stu doesn't seem to be listening.

"Everything on the body goes to the coroner's office, but we have possession of items found apart from the body. Those include a wedding ring and part of a white shirt." He takes two photographs from Detective Schwartz and shows them to Stu. Do you recognize these?"

While Stu studies the photos, Detective Schwartz gazes around the room. He takes his time as he looks at everything. The man gives me the creeps.

"It looks sort of like Sarah's ring," says Stu, "but I can't be sure. And I don't recognize the blouse at all."

"Could you come to the department, please, and identify the ring? You don't have to do it today; tomorrow would be fine."

Stu nods his head, not looking at the detective.

"We'd also like to have her toothbrush. For the DNA testing."

"Yes." Stu just sits there, his face expressionless.

"Could you get it for us, please?"

Stu seems to be frozen in place.

"Stu?" Hank puts a hand on his shoulder. "You want me to go upstairs for you?"

Stu shakes his head, as if he's trying to wake up. "No. No, I'll get it."

When he has left the room, Detective Schultz asks, "Mr. Arrowby? Will you be able to keep an eye on him?"

"I'm right next door and we're good friends. I'll see if he wants to stay at my house tonight."

Whoopee! That would scotch the romantic dinner with Ann Dimples.

"I have a question," Hank says. "How could it possibly be Sarah? You say the body is badly decomposed, but it's only been three and a half weeks since she disappeared."

"The weather," says Schwartz. "A body can decompose quite rapidly in hot weather, and we've had more than our share of that this past month."

"I see." Hank looks away and I can see his jaw muscles twitching.

Stu returns with the toothbrush, looking more alert than when he left.

"Thank you, sir," says Holcomb, holding open a plastic bag for the toothbrush. "Now, is there anything you want to ask us?"

"Yes. I...I suppose she was murdered. Can they tell how she was killed?"

"The autopsy showed a skull fracture."

Detective Holcomb has a way of looking at you that is even creepier than Schwartz. He has dark brown eyes, smaller than Hank's, and his face shows no expression. He might as well be a blank wall that talks.

"Anything else you want to ask?"

Stu shakes his head, still not looking anybody in the face, and sits down.

After a few more sympathetic words the detectives leave their cards with Stu and let themselves out. Stu doesn't budge from his chair, so Hank pulls his own directly in front of him and puts both hands on Stu's knees. "Maybe it isn't Sarah," he says.

Stu slowly shakes his head. "I know it's her. I know it. Oh, God."

Without warning, he breaks into sobs, tears streaming down his cheeks. He hangs onto Hank, body shaking. Stuart Fetzler, dapper, handsome, composed gentleman, is a mess. Hank holds him for a long time, until the sobbing ceases.

I'm not in such great shape, myself, and what I really want is to be alone with Hank and feel the touch of his hand on my body. My wish is granted when at last Stu asks to be left alone. Hank is reluctant to leave him, but Stu assures him that he will be all right.

Not until we are back home does Hank allow himself to cry without restraint. It wrenches my gut to see him like this and I find myself whining.

"It's all right, Sam," he says. "It's all right. You don't understand, old boy."

The hell I don't. We all know it's highly likely the body is Sarah's. Beautiful, generous, sweet, thoughtful, loving Sarah. It's not fair.

I whine again.

Since all the food for tonight's dinner has been bought and much of the prepping done, Hank apparently has decided not to cancel the meal.

When Ann arrives she takes one look at Hank's face and says, "Hank, what's the matter?"

"I didn't think it showed," says Hank. "We've had bad news." He takes her hand and leads her to the kitchen. "They found a body."

"Oh, no." Ann's eyes glisten and she puts both hands on Hank's shoulders. "Oh, no," she repeats. "I'm so sorry, Hank."

"It's possible that it's not Sarah, but in my gut I know it is."

Ann wraps her arms around Hank's ribs and he holds her tightly, rubbing her back. They stand that way awhile, until Hank pulls back his head, looks intently into her face, then kisses her passionately.

I have a bad feeling about this.

Without warning, Hank scoops her up and carries her down the hall to his bedroom.

"First I have to take care of the dog," he tells her.

Damn! Not the studio! I haven't even had my steak.

Being black and relatively small, I can be hard to spot, so I hunker down behind a living room chair, but Hank finds me, anyway, and he matter-of-factly shoves me into the studio.

It's all a result of the first time Hank took a woman to bed after I'd come to live with him. I had curled up at the side of the bed and at first didn't pay much attention to the noises and thrashing around above me. Eventually, some interesting odors wafted my way, arousing my curiosity, so I sat up. Right in front of my nose a pinkish-white, soft mound of flesh rolled back and forth. Trying to get a better whiff, I sniffed it.

You never heard such screaming in your life. You would think I'd stuck a knife to her. As for Hank, I was afraid he'd have a stroke, his face was so red. Yelling obscenities the entire way, he threw me into the studio, and left me there the rest of the night. I could hear him trying to pacify the lady, but she would have none of it and it wasn't long before the front door slammed. It wasn't fair of Hank to be so angry with me. After all, how was I to know there was such a thing as sex etiquette?

CHAPTER 13

Early Monday morning Hank lets me out to pee and fixes my breakfast, but it's another three hours before he and Her Nibs manage to concoct their own meal. With all the hugging and kissing, it's a miracle they get it onto the table at all. I'm so disgusted I plop myself down in the living room for a snooze, awakening only when Ann leaves. While Hank sees her to her car, I spot Stu on the way to his mailbox and I bound through the bushes to his side. He squats down and ruffles me behind the ears.

I look into Stu's eyes and the whites are crisscrossed with red lines. Below his eyes he has grown dark pouches.

"You're a great dog, you know that?" Stu smells good.

Waving to Ann as she drives down the street, Hank walks over to us. "You okay?" he asks Stu.

"Yeah. Sam makes me feel better." I shake myself with pleasure.

Stu raises his eyebrows and nods in the direction of Ann's retreating car. "Company?"

"Yep." Instead of elaborating, Hank changes the subject and asks Stu if he's heard anymore from the Sheriffs Department.

"Yes, actually. They called half an hour ago and want me down there to identify jewelry. I'm having trouble getting up the nerve to go. Silly, I guess."

"Nothing silly about it, Stu. Listen, why don't I drive you?"

Stu protests, but Hank will have none of it, and in truth I believe Stu is grateful for the support.

With me in the back seat of the Volkswagen, we drive the ten miles or so to downtown San Jose where Hank has trouble locating the Sheriff's Department. Stu says it's on Younger St., but the guys are confused between its location and the San Jose Police Department, so we meander up and down side streets, taking what Hank refers to as "the scenic route." When they do find the Sheriffs Department, they park in a shaded area where I'm left to my own amusement in the car, much to my disappointment.

Several pigeons converge on a spot in the parking lot where somebody dropped part of a hot dog bun. Heads bobbing, they peck at crumbs and squabble with each other over the larger pieces. I yearn to rush at them and send them flying, but I'm locked in. It is frustrating to be so close, yet not able to get at them. A large woman in a red 49ers T-shirt and extremely tight black pants approaches. She is carrying a baby and holding the hand of a little boy, who spots the pigeons, wrests his hand away, and charges at the birds. I couldn't have done a better job myself. I can hear the flapping of their wings as the pigeons frantically take off for the safety of the skies. The woman yells at the little boy, which I think is uncalled for. After all, he was only doing what I would have done myself.

That amusement over, I shove my nose out the window, hoping for some exotic odors. I smell hot dogs, the aroma wafting my way from a street vendor's cart on the corner, and I also detect burritos and tacos. I find myself drooling, so I pull my head inside, hoping that Hank won't notice the streaks on the window. Bored, I stretch out on the back seat for a snooze.

When the men return an hour later, Stu's shoulders are drooping like wet laundry. He shuffles past the parked cars, looking down at his feet, his hands in his pockets. Hank pats him on the back as he gets into the car. Hank inserts the key into the ignition, but he doesn't start the engine.

"You want to talk about it?" he asks.

"I'm sorry," says Stu, "that you had to hang around in the lobby all that time. I was hoping they'd let you come in with me, but no dice." He sighs and rubs his hands over his face.

"What's it like in there?"

"Schwartz took me up to the third floor and through a room of cubicles. There are interview rooms along the sides, so we went into one of those. It was small, Spartan—you know, like what you'd see in a movie. It had one of those one-way mirror things and I assume video cameras, but they weren't obvious. Tape recorder, of course.

"Shortly after we sat down, Holcomb came in with two plastic bags, one with a wedding ring and the other with torn, dirty clothing. I recognized the ring as Sarah's and it really took my breath away. I expected they'd give me the ring, but they're holding it as part of the evidence. Next they tell me that the crime lab has made a positive identification based on dental work. It is Sarah." Stu's voice breaks and Hank closes his eyes. "Then they inform me of my rights and repeat questions they've already asked more than once. I was starting to answer when it hit me: I need a lawyer. A criminal lawyer, for crissake. This can't be happening to me." Stu twists his body to face Hank. "Do you know any lawyers?"

"Jeez, no, Stu. Pete oughta know, though. We'll call him."

I take notice of the "we" in Hank's response. Stu is lucky to have him as a friend; Hank goes all out for people he cares about. Sometimes I worry about that.

"Would you do me a big favor, Hank? I've talked with my father-in-law twice, but he's so broken up he can hardly talk. Could you possibly go to Mendocino and see him for me? I know it's a lot to ask."

"No problem. I'll call Jack and see what's a good day for me to visit. I'm glad I can do something."

And I'm glad I'll be traveling again.

The following morning we're up early because Hank is way behind in his pottery work. I overheard him on the phone last evening with Stu, and from what I could make out it sounded as if Stu had found an attorney. Somebody named Brewster.

Hank opens the *Mercury News* and sharply draws in his breath. "How could they find out so fast?" he mutters under his breath. By 8:00 breakfast is over, dishes are cleaned up, and Hank has envelopes to put in the mailbox. When he opens the front door, we are both bowled over by the sight next door. Backed into the Fetzler driveway is a mammoth black SUV, and between it and the street is a Sheriffs Department car. On the street in front of the house sits a black Ford Crown Victoria. I spot two guys in coveralls just entering the house and a couple of deputies stand in the front yard.

"What the hell?" says Hank.

When he moves to the mailbox I dash through the bushes into Stu's yard and up to one of the deputies, a tall friendly-looking guy. A strong odor emanates from his pant legs, which I investigate carefully. Hmmm. Female. Large. Probably a Labrador.

"Hey, pooch," says the deputy.

"Sammy, come here!" shouts Hank, hurriedly limping toward us.

He apologizes, but the deputy reassures him. "Don't worry about it. Dogs are dogs. I have a yellow Lab and your dog probably smells her." I knew it.

Stu and Detective Holcomb step out from the house and I don't like the expression on Stu's face. His jaw is so tight it looks as if you'd need a crowbar to pry it open. "I'll be next door," he says. He stomps across the yard and right into our house, with Hank and me following.

Once inside, Stu paces around the living room. "I can't believe it. Just one day after Sarah's body is identified and already they serve me with a search warrant." Pace, pace. "I knew they'd want the car back right away, but search the house?" Pace, pace. "Jesus, they must think I killed her." He stops abruptly. "I need to call Brewster."

Stu whips out his cell phone and leaves a message for his lawyer, then resumes his pacing. I can tell it is driving Hank nuts, because shortly he suggests that Stu take me for a walk.

"That's a good idea. I need some air. Listen, Hank, keep an eye on what's happening at the house, okay? Oh, and if that reporter Dan What's-his-name, shows up, tell him you don't know where I am. He called me yesterday afternoon."

It seems strange to have someone other than Hank on the end of my leash, but Stu makes a good substitute. He doesn't jerk my chain and he allows me to spend as much time sniffing as I want. He's a little distracted, though, and almost leads me into the path of a Toyota Tundra when we cross Carlton Ave. The driver looks familiar, but Stu doesn't notice. We meander through unfamiliar neighborhoods for over an hour and I'm feeling uneasy. Is Stu lost?

Relief floods over me when I realize we are headed toward home, but it's short lived; the Tundra is parked on our street and now I recognize the driver—Windsor Huddleston. Stu pays no attention, his eyes on his house across the street. For a moment he stops in front of Mrs. Crawford's place, giving me a chance to spot Crabby peering out from behind her living room drapes. No doubt she'll soon be ensconced on her front porch, working on her Christmas egg ornaments and enjoying the show in front of her.

The tall deputy is leaning against the van and I'm wishing Stu would approach him so that I could get another whiff of the yellow Lab; instead, Stu simply stands under Hank's magnolia tree, watching.

Hank soon joins us, taking the leash from Stu. "Good walk?" he asks.

"It helped," Stu says.

"I called Jack and he says Thursday would be best for him. Oh, and while you were gone they took away Sarah's car. You're not surprised, are you?"

"No. I just wish they'd get out of my house."

"Don't blame you." Hank looks up and down the street, his eyes narrowing when he notices the white Tundra. "Is that who I think it is? What the hell is he doing here?"

"Who?" asks Stu, looking bewildered, but Hank is already limping quickly toward the truck and doesn't answer.

With nobody on the other end of my leash, I lunge through the bushes and up to the deputy's trousers.

"You again?" he says, grabbing me.

I'm curious about what's happening inside Stu's house, but the deputy hangs onto me until Stu appears around the bushes.

"How long are you people going to be here?" Stu says.

"I can't say, sir. It may take all day, even two days."

"Well, please tell Lieutenant Holcomb that I have an appointment with my lawyer and I'll be returning later." Stu takes my leash from the deputy and pulls me home to Hank, who is approaching his front yard. Behind him I observe Huddleston's truck driving off.

"What was that all about?" says Stu.

"Windsor Huddleston," says Hank. "He saw me coming and took off. Why is he nosing around here, I'd like to know."

"Forget him." Stu's cell phone rings and he flips the cover, notes the number, and flips it back. "I have a 10:00 appointment with Philip Brewster. Since he's not returning my call I think I'll head on down to his office early— that is, if those guys over there will let me have my car." He shakes his head at Hank. "It's freaky, Hank, having strangers prowling all over your house."

Hank claps Stu on the back as he turns away, and I try to imagine what it must be like to learn your wife was murdered and then have to be considered a possible suspect. Stu is one of the nice guys of this world. It isn't fair.

Half an hour later I'm lying on the cool concrete of the studio, watching Hank set up his work, when the doorbell rings. I race ahead of Hank through the house, plant my paws up on the living room window sill, and check out the stranger at the front door. The guy is older than Hank, with a leathery face and a pot belly. He looks away, his squinty eyes scanning the neighborhood, and immediately I don't like him.

"My name is Dan O'Keefe," he says, handing Hank a card when the door is opened. "I'm a reporter with the *Mercury News*."

Hank looks at the card, then back at the man, and I know he's trying to make up his mind whether or not he should talk to him.

"I'd like to ask you a few questions, if you don't mind," says O'Keefe. He gives Hank a forced smile which no doubt is meant to be reassuring, but personally I wouldn't give him the time of day. "May I come in?"

"I guess so," says Hank, opening the door.

O'Keefe walks right past him into the living room, not even bothering to wipe his shoes on the doormat. I'll bet Hank is already sorry he let this character into his house.

"Where should I sit?" asks O'Keefe.

Hank sighs and motions the reporter to a chair. I'm amused, because it's an oversized club chair, uncomfortable unless you're a big person, and this guy is short.

"I suppose you're here because of the Fetzler murder," says Hank.

"Correct." O'Keefe tries to sit back in the chair, but there's way too much space, so he's forced to sit on the edge.

I saunter over to him and pretend to be friendly. The smell of tobacco assaults my nose, so I return to Hank's side and settle down.

"Cute dog," says O'Keefe, whipping out a small notebook. "Your name, sir?"

"Hank Arrowby." O'Keefe clicks his ballpoint pen and checks the spelling of Hank's name. Oh, great, Hank. Now you'll be reading your name in the paper,

"Profession, Mr. Arrowby?"

"Retired firefighter. Now I'm a potter."

"Is there a Mrs. Arrowby?"

"Nope."

"How long have you lived in this house?"

"Look, Mr. O'Keefe, I can save us both a lot of time. Stuart Fetzler is a good friend of mine and no way am I going to talk about him."

O'Keefe seems to be trying to strike a casual pose, but since he can't lean back, he turns a bit sideways and rests his back on the arm of the chair. If Hank thought he would get rid of this reporter quickly, he was mistaken.

"I can understand your reluctance, but you should realize that this is an opportunity to do him a favor—to let the public know he's an upstanding citizen, if that's what he is."

There is a long pause while O'Keefe gives Hank plenty of time to chew on what he just said. The guy is no dummy.

Hank sighs. "I suppose that's true."

"So, back to my question. How long have you lived here?"

"Fifteen years."

"And how long have the Fetzlers lived next door?"

"About ten years or so."

O'Keefe scribbles Hank's answers on his pad. He must use some sort of shorthand.

"You said Stuart Fetzler is a good friend. What about his wife? Did you know Sarah Fetzler well?"

"Yes. Sarah and I both like to cook and the two of us would often try out recipes together. In fact, we had dinner here the night before she disappeared. You couldn't meet a nicer person than Sarah Fetzler. Friendly, warm, funny, just a great lady."

"How did she seem that last night?"

"Same as always. There was nothing unusual."

"How would you describe their marriage?"

"If they had any problems, I sure didn't know it. They made a great couple. Really great. You can ask anybody in this neighborhood and you'll get the same answer, I guarantee."

"And Stuart Fetzler? What has been his reaction to his wife's death?"

"What do you think? How would you feel if your wife was murdered?" Hank is swollen with indignation.

O'Keefe appears not to notice. "Everyone reacts differently. I'm asking you how he has responded. Has he been depressed? Angry? Withdrawn? Stoic? What?"

Hank pauses before answering. "Probably all of the above. The man is devastated. What more can I say?"

"You live in a nice neighborhood. Do the neighbors get along?"

"It's a friendly place."

"I understand Sarah was a family therapist and Stuart is a college teacher. What do you know about their professional reputations?"

Abruptly, Hank stands up. "Look, I've said all I'm going to say about the Fetzlers. They had a good marriage. Everybody liked them both and we're all still in shock about Sarah's murder. Somewhere out there is a killer."

In no hurry to get up, O'Keefe flips the page of his little notebook and scribbles a few more words. I notice the nicotine stains on his fingers.

"Okay, Mr. Arrowby." O'Keefe pushes himself up from the chair with a little grunt. The man is out of shape. "Thank you for your time."

After seeing him out, Hank returns to his pottery, but his heart doesn't seem to be in it. He unwraps a wet piece, picks up a tool, then stares into space. It's like that the rest of the day: work a little; stare a little; sigh a lot. At the end of the afternoon Hank puts down a shaping tool and says, "I need to go where her body was found."

CHAPTER 14

I can tell that Hank has something on his mind because he stares into space while drinking his morning cup of coffee and when he slips the choke chain over my neck for our walk he doesn't bother talking to me.

Outdoors the sun is already blinding bright. We cross the street just as Crabby opens her front door. Hank waves to her.

"Keep that dog clear of my rose bush, Hank." Not even a "hello" or a "how are you." What a woman.

"And good morning to you, too, Mrs. Crawford." Hank chuckles and loosens his grip on the leash as we pass by the precious rose bush. I ignore it. Why would anyone want such a plant? It's full of thorns.

Already the air is heating up, but the grass in the park remains cool and soothes my paws. Opossum scent lingers on the blades near an imposing oak tree, so of course I have to spend extra time there. Hank must be lost in his own thoughts, because he lets me sniff and roll as long as I want in the spot. I don't know why I feel compelled to transfer opossum essence onto my own shoulders. It must be a primitive drive, which fact disturbs me, since I consider myself rather highly evolved.

On our way back we near the Hoyt's front yard where Mrs. Hoyt is watering petunias at the edge of the driveway. At the sight of us, she straightens up and raises her arm to get Hank's attention. The flab of her upper arm flops from side to side,

"Hank," she calls, "whenever it's convenient, could you give me some advice on a bowl I bought at the flea market? I think it might be worth something and I value your opinion."

"Mrs. Hoyt, you know I'm not..."

"Please. It's Freda. And yes, dear, I realize you're not an appraiser, but you do know artistic pottery when you see it."

I'm sure Hank is gritting his teeth. Mrs. Hoyt is forever snagging him to examine some dumb piece or another, and Hank is too polite to refuse. I think her real motive is to have a conversation with a normal man. Lord knows her son is not up to the task.

"Maybe later today. I'll try." Hank jerks the leash and we hurry home.

After we've each satisfied our thirsts, Hank rummages around in his desk, swearing periodically, until he unearths an old map. He mutters something about a road that Pete described to him. I hear the words "Highway Nine" and "Skyline" and it dawns on me that Hank is talking about the area where Sarah's body was found. Don't tell me we're going there.

It's almost 10:00 when we leave, but instead of going straight through Los Gatos to Saratoga, Hank turns onto Los Gatos Boulevard, and I realize he'll end up on Main Street, right in front of the gallery where Ann Schaefer no doubt is at work. Nuts.

I'm in a funk, so I turn around in the back seat and look out the rear window instead of the front. Watching the scenery recede rather than advance toward me is unsettling. I feel as if life is passing me by before I've had a chance to enjoy it. I turn around again.

Hank finds a parking space directly in front of the gallery. I'm hoping he'll leave me in the car so that I'm not forced to be with that woman, but of course he makes me go with him.

"What's the matter with you?" he says.

Inside, he and Ann embrace as if they hadn't seen each other for years. There is a long kiss. I look away and stare at the nearest piece of art: a purple vase with ceramic flowers in the shape of human faces. Even looking at the kiss is better than this.

"I wasn't expecting to see you today," says Ann in her perky little voice.

"You were on my route," says Hank, "so I figured I might as well drop in and say hi."

"Are you doing business in Los Gatos?"

"No. Actually, I'm going to check out the area where Sarah's body was found."

I knew it.

"How are you going to find it?"

"Pete told me where the road is. It's not marked because people keep taking down the sign, but I know how far it is from Highway 9 and he said what to look for. I'll find it."

"But why? Are you trying to play detective?"

Hank shrugs his shoulders. "I don't know, Ann. To tell the truth, I don't even know what I'm looking for. I just need to do it."

Ann frowns and lays a hand on Hank's arm. "I know you want to help find her killer, but that's not your job, Hank."

Perhaps Miss Wonderful has more sense than I've given her credit for.

"Maybe not. Anyway, I'll feel better after I've done this."

Not long after, Hank has me back in the VW. We take the long way around through Saratoga, where Hank stops at a store, and finally we begin the mountain climb, snaking our way up to the junction with Skyline where Hank turns sharply to the left. We haven't gone far before he slows the car, checking the occasional road on the right. Ahead of us a familiar white Toyota pulls out from a road, causing Hank to slow down abruptly.

"Hey!" he says. "That's Hud's truck."

To my surprise, Hank follows Hud, keeping well back and allowing a weather-beaten old Dodge to come between them. Hud turns left onto Bear Creek Road, the Dodge doing the same.

"Good," says Hank, joining the procession. "Less chance he'll notice me."

We twist our way down the mountain and Hud is quite a distance ahead once we hit Highway 17. I'm thinking he will elude us, but Hank manages to keep him in sight in spite of heavy traffic. Once again we climb, around "Valley Surprise," past Summit Road, down Soquel grade, twisting and turning our way toward Santa Cruz.

"For awhile I thought he might be going home," says Hank. "I know he lives on Summit Road." He looks at me in the rear view mirror. "You okay, Sammy? You like it when I talk to you?" If he only knew.

Hud takes the exit to Highway 1. Hank follows so far back that for awhile I think we've lost him, but we spot him turning onto the street that leads toward Natural Bridges. Instead of going to the state park, however, he makes a left onto West Cliff Drive and stops at one of the pull-outs. Hank turns into a side street, and parks so that he has a view of Hud's truck.

At this distance I can see that Hud, who has left his truck and is watching the crashing waves, turns to greet a paunchy middle-aged man who walks with a cane. They shake hands and sit on a wooden bench along the cliff. Hank pulls out the small binoculars he keeps in the glove compartment and zeroes in on the pair. I get a blow-by-blow description while Hank talks.

"Who is that guy? He looks familiar. Hud is giving him something. Looks like a package. No, a manila envelope. Damn, I can't see well enough.

Wish I had your eyes, Sammy. The guy is taking things out and looking at them. What the hell is Hud up to?"

I can tell that Hud is talking because he gestures with his hands; then he stops and looks out at the ocean. When his head swivels our way Hank drops the binoculars and pretends to be checking something in the glove compartment. I'm thinking this is ridiculous. Why not just approach Windsor Huddleston and ask him why he was on Skyline near the crime scene? Then Hud could introduce Hank to the stranger and Hank would know what the meeting was all about. Humans tend to complicate their lives unnecessarily.

Next thing I know, Hank is shoving me off the seat and we hunker down until Hud and the stranger have parted ways. I'm hoping this is the end of the pseudo-private eye game and we can go play ball on a beach, but Hank isn't finished playing Sherlock Homes. He backs up the VW, puts it into first gear, and lurches forward so quickly that I'm thrown around the back seat.

"Sorry, old boy. No time to lose."

When I've regained my balance I see that we're retracing our route and soon we're headed back over the mountain on Highway 17. I can't see Hud's truck, but Hank apparently can, because we turn off onto Summit Road. Hank slows the car and we cruise along for about a mile.

"There's the truck," he says. "Looks like he's already inside his house."

Hud's home looks recently remodeled with double-paned windows, a fresh paint job in a beige color, and a roof with solar panels. There is fire danger in these mountains, and Hud has no foliage close to the house. The yard looks neat and well cared for.

We casually drive past the place like a couple out for a Sunday drive. This is embarrassing. I'm relieved when Hank continues along Summit to Old Santa Cruz Highway and we take this longer route down the mountain to connect again with Highway 17. Perhaps now we can spend the rest of the day like normal people.

Hank's mind must be far away because he misses Branham Lane and we turn onto Carlton, bringing us to our street from the southern approach. This means we must pass the Hoyt house and I'm sure Hank is ruing his mistake. Mrs. Hoyt waves to us from the front yard where she's deadheading some sort of bush.

"Aw, hell," says Hank, waving back. "I may as well get this over with"

We each make a pit stop at our house—Hank in the bathroom and me at the magnolia tree in the front yard. Then it's on to Mrs. Hoyt and her precious pot.

"Thank you so much, Hank, for doing this," says Mrs. Hoyt, her jowly face flushed from her stooping over with her gardening. "I promise not to take up much of your time."

"No problem," says Hank.

Yeah, right.

Inside the house Mrs. Hoyt leaves us in the living room while she fetches her new possession. Hank looks over Brick's latest addition to the décor. He stops short at a large collage hanging to the right of the fireplace. The creation consists mainly of belt buckles, jewelry, tin can lids, and a variety of connecting strings and twine. Something in the collage has attracted his attention. Hank peers closely at the object and his face pales.

"My God," he whispers. "That's Sarah's butterfly pin."

Returning with a garishly decorated bowl, Mrs. Hoyt beams at Hank. "That's Arthur's latest creation. I think it's the best he's done. Do you like it?"

Hank almost chokes on his words. "Oh, yeah, yeah, it's real good."

"Now sit down and look at this closely," says Mrs. Hoyt, thrusting the bowl at Hank and motioning him into a chair. "Good boy," she says to me, patting me on the head, but I don't pay much attention because I'm focused on Hank.

He turns the bowl over in his hands. It's an ugly thing, bright green covered with flowers painted in red, purple, blue, yellow, and white. Something has been glued to the centers of the flowers that make them sparkle. Hank checks the bottom and runs his fingers along the rim. "It's interesting," he says, "but it's not valuable." Seeing Mrs. Hoyt's crestfallen face, he adds, "But you must remember, Freda, art appreciation is a subjective thing. What's important is whether or not you like a piece. Enjoy it, regardless of its worth."

Hank's eyes go to the collage by the fireplace. "Take Arthur's work, for example. He's creating it, you're enjoying it. That's all that matters."

As Hank stands up to return to the collage, Brick materializes at the doorway. For a solid person built like a tank, the man can certainly move quietly. Today he's wearing baggy camouflage pants and a Harley-Davidson T-shirt with the sleeves cut off. He looks as if he just woke up, because his eyes are puffy and the left side of his face appears to have a crease in it.

"Why are you looking at that?" he says.

"Now, Arthur." Mrs. Hoyt is quick to intrude. "Pictures are meant to be looked at. You should be proud that Hank is interested in your work."

Hank has his face close to the collage. "Where do you find this stuff, Arthur?"

Brick nears Hank, watching him closely. "Why should you care where I find it?"

Hank's nose is inches from Sarah's pin. "This butterfly pin; I've seen it before."

"So what?"

"Sarah Fetzler has a pin like this."

"I repeat, so what?"

Brick is so close to Hank now that I'm afraid he'll squash him against the wall. Hank backs up and turns away.

"Just wondering, that's all." His jaw muscles twitch.

We take our leave with Mrs. Hoyt all a-twitter over our rapid exit and Brick scowling like a drill sergeant behind her. At home Hank whips out his wallet, retrieves a business card, and is on the phone before I've had a chance to settle on my blanket in the corner.

"Detective Holcomb? Hank Arrowby, the Fetzler's neighbor. I have some information for you. Please call me back." His words are hurried and I can feel the excitement he's choking back.

Hank fixes his belated lunch, but only eats half of it, staring off into space between bites. I know better than to expect him to share the leftovers, so I lie down in the living room and spend the next hour dozing while Hank does paperwork in the den. My sleep is restless, because I feel as if something is about to happen, but I don't know what.

Late in the afternoon the doorbell rings. "Don't tell me O'Keefe is back," says Hank as he walks past me.

It's Detectives Holcomb and Schwartz.

"I thought you'd call me back," says Hank. "I didn't expect you to come here."

"We were planning to interview you, anyway," says Detective Holcomb, "so this seemed like a good time."

Hank leads them into the living room and I plant myself at Hank's side where I can watch the detectives easily. Holcomb sets his recorder on the coffee table and Hank nods his permission.

"What is it you wanted to tell us, Mr. Arrowby?"

Hank recounts his experience at Brick's house. He describes the butterfly pin and explains why he is so sure that it is Sarah's. Again, as Hank talks, I am unsettled by the lack of expression on Holcomb's face and the way his eyes bore into Hank's. I wonder if it bothers Hank, too.

"I may be over-reacting, but it does seem strange that a possession of Sarah's should suddenly appear in a new creation of Brick's, I mean, Arthur's. And he was plenty angry when I commented on it."

"You said that he makes collages out of scraps. Is this the first time he's used something that you've recognized?"

"I haven't looked closely at his stuff before."

I glance at Detective Schwartz and notice that he's scanning the room in the same way that he did at Stu's place. These guys mean business.

"What can you tell us about Arthur Hoyt?"

Hank shrugs his shoulders. "Not much. He's lived in this neighborhood longer than I have. Lives with his mother and keeps to himself. He doesn't have a job that I know of, just works on his collages. I don't know what his problem is, his diagnosis, I mean, but I've always considered him harmless."

"Do you know if he had any contact with Sarah Fetzler?"

"Just when they'd meet in the neighborhood. Sarah felt sorry for him, I think. She would go out of her way to speak to Brick and was always very respectful of him."

"All right." Holcomb readjusts his position in the chair. It's the same one that O'Keefe sat in, but the detective fits in it much better. "Tell me about yourself. How long have you lived here?"

Detective Holcomb asks many of the same questions that the reporter did, and Hank answers them with some edginess. He frowns and his jaw muscles flex. Hank would never make a detective: all his emotions show on his face.

"You know," he says, "I've answered the same questions for a reporter. Why don't I just make a recording and hand out copies to everyone?"

Knowing Hank as I do, I think he's aiming for a little humor, but it's wasted on old Stoneface. If Holcomb were to smile, his face would crack.

"You seem to be bothered by my questions, Mr. Arrowby." The laser eyes fasten onto Hank's.

Great, Hank. You're fast becoming a suspect.

Hank seems to realize his mistake, because his tone is at once apologetic. "I'm sorry, Detective. I know you're only doing your job. I think I'm just angry because Sarah was murdered and I'm anxious for her killer to be found now. Ask me anything you want." He relaxes and leans back in the chair.

Holcomb remains impassive as he continues with questions, including asking about Hank's leg and his work history.

"Sarah was a great help to me after I was injured," says Hank. "She took wonderful care of my dog and brought meals when I returned home. She was a true friend."

"Did you have a sexual relationship with her?"

Hank is so startled that he jerks, and then he bursts into laughter. "No! We made meals together, we didn't make love."

I'm so disgusted with Holcomb that I try some laser stares of my own, but he ignores me. I've noticed that he carries no dog smell on him, which is not surprising, because no self-respecting dog wants an owner who is emotionless.

"You've made it clear that you think the Fetzlers had a good marriage. Did Sarah ever express a fear of anybody?"

Hank shakes his head. "No"

"What were her normal activities, at least as far as you could tell?"

"She was a family therapist, as you know, and she worked long hours. She'd go into the office around 9:00 or 9:30 and come home around 7:00 p.m. Some nights she worked until 9:00 p.m."

"Weekends?"

"She spent a lot of time gardening, and she was a gourmet cook. Often she and I would cook together."

"Who else do you think we should talk to?"

"Miriam Weinberg, her business partner." Hank sighs and squirms in his chair. "And then there's Hud. Windsor Huddleston. Some years back he had an affair with Sarah."

"We know about both of them."

Hank's eyebrows shoot up.

Holcomb explains, "They were interviewed when Sarah went missing. We'll interview them again, of course. Anybody else?"

"None that I can think of."

"We'll interview all the neighbors. Is there anyone other than Mr. Hoyt you think we should pay special attention to?"

"Nope." There is a little twitch at the corner of Hank's mouth and I know he's thinking of Crabby Crawford. He's probably imagining the fun that Holcomb will have interviewing her.

"All right." Holcomb shuts off the recorder and gets up with a grunt. "Thank you for your time, Mr. Arrowby. Feel free to give us a call if anything else occurs to you that you think we should know, even if it doesn't seem very important. You have my card, right?"

"Yep," says Hank. He escorts Holcomb and Schwartz to the door and I follow.

"Well behaved dog," says Holcomb.

I may have to revise my opinion of the man.

Late in the evening the phone rings, and from the way Hank's face brightens when he answers it I know the caller is Ann.

"No, I didn't get to see the place," he says, "because Windsor Huddleston drove out of that road just as I was approaching, so I followed him to Santa Cruz and..." Hank throws an arm up in the air, as if he were trying to stop what Ann was saying.

"No, no, he didn't see me." Pause. "Because I know he didn't, okay?" Pause. "Listen, Ann, I'm not going to do anything foolish. Stop worrying." Pause. "Yes, yes, I'll be careful."

They talk a little longer, and when Hank hangs up, the joy that lit up his face when he first heard Ann's voice is no longer there.

CHAPTER 15

I sit alertly on the front lawn, watching Hank stuff a duffel bag, heavy jacket, my dog dishes, a bag of dog food, and other assorted gear into the VW. I'm not the only one paying close attention to his activity, of course; Crabby has him in her sights.

"Yoo hoo, Hank," she calls. "Are you going away?"

"Yep." Hank doesn't look Crabby's way when he responds, probably because he does not want to get engaged in a conversation with her.

"Will you be gone long? Do you want me to do anything for you at the house?"

"Nope."

"I'll keep an eye out, anyway."

Of course she will. If she could, Crabby would remove her eyes and plant them on a pole right at the curb. That way, she would be able to snoop on more of the neighborhood, instead of being restricted to the view from her front porch.

"Okay, Sammy," says Hank, "hop in the car."

We're off and running. In no time at all, we have left Interstate 85 and are rolling along through the golden hills of Interstate 280. This is my first experience north of the San Jose area, and the excitement has me panting. I rest my nose on the edge of the window that Hank has opened a crack, hoping for new olfactory stimulation, but all I get is wind stinging my nose.

In an hour's time we approach the outskirts of San Francisco and I'm torn between looking out the window and hunkering down on the seat. The sights and sounds of an energetic major city are both intriguing and terrifying. There are so many cars, merging and then exiting lanes, and the pace seems faster, although that may be my imagination. Hank gets in the wrong lane a couple of times, which adds to my anxiety. I relax more once we are on 19th Avenue and have to stop at traffic lights. It gives me a chance to study the houses that line the street. Some of them are quite colorful with shades of blue and yellow and pink, and they are smack against each other with no space in between. A few have wrought iron balconies. Most of them have only one garage, which is right at the sidewalk. Some people park their cars half in the street and half on the sidewalk. A streetcar line runs in the middle.

"Hey, Sam, get a load of that Newfie taking his owner for a walk." Hank points to a giant black dog that closely resembles a bear. At the other end of the bear's taut leash clings a determined and curvaceous blonde woman. I'm hoping Hank doesn't get some hair-brained idea that he should stop the car and help her out. Fortunately, he just laughs and continues to thread his way through the traffic on 19th Avenue. I lower myself onto the seat, thinking maybe I'll take a nap, but Hank has other ideas.

"Look, Sam, we're on the bridge! It's the Golden Gate."

Pushing myself up, I'm disappointed to see that there is nothing golden about the Golden Gate Bridge. It's a rusty red color, of all things. Nice cables, though, and from the other side the view of the landmark bridge with shining San Francisco skyscrapers in the distance is pretty darn nice. Beats a neighborhood walk any day.

We cruise north on 101 through some industrial towns, interspersed with rural land, and at one point I spot a group of extremely large, black and white dogs. No, they are not dogs. Strange, ungainly creatures with brush-tipped, long skinny tails that flick back and forth across their flanks. Each one has a hairless bag under its belly.

Sam notices me in the rear view mirror. "See the cows, Sam? Bet you'd like to investigate them up close."

I get a whiff through the open window. No thanks.

It's back for a snooze on the seat, until I'm awakened by the change in speed and the sharp turn of the car. We have pulled into a parking lot near a cafe with outdoor seating. It's a cute little place with large pots of colorful flowers around the patio. Each of the round metal tables has a green and white striped umbrella on it. One of the tables is unoccupied and Hank stakes a claim on it, hooking my leash to one of the legs. He brings my portable water bowl, then goes inside to place his order.

I look around at the other patrons. A neatly dressed lady with gray hair pulled back in a ponytail sits primly at the table next to us. She is eating a large hamburger, taking small bites and delicately nipping off the lettuce leaves that protrude from the bun. I salivate and have to turn away.

At our other side, a family of four noisily downs burgers and fries. A toddler in a booster seat mostly plays with his food, occasionally flinging French fries onto the ground. Some fries head my way, but not close enough to grab, leaving me incredibly frustrated. I can drag the table only about two inches. I am saved by the appearance of Hank bearing a basket of fish and chips.

"Guess what, Sam. They keep a jar of dog biscuits in there. Here you go."

He flips me the treat and down it goes. I suppose he thinks I should be pacified with this, but all it does is whet my appetite, especially when I watch him crunch down on that crispy fish and I smell that delectable grease. Another French fry from next door flips our way. So near and yet so far.

Before long, the family packs up, along with most of the other customers, leaving us and the prim little lady. She looks our way and Hank smiles and nods at her. She smiles shyly back.

A chunky middle-aged woman wearing a green and white striped apron emerges from the cafe. "Would you like another coke, Doris?" she asks our neighbor.

"No, thank you. I'm finished. Thank you ever so much."

Slowly, the woman rises from her chair and walks over to the side of the building. There she claims a grocery store cart filled with bulging plastic bags and a sleeping bag. She is a small lady and the cart looks too heavy for her to push, but she manages to maneuver it around the tables and onto the sidewalk. With great dignity she walks away, never looking back.

Hank cocks an eyebrow at the waitress and she anticipates his question. "Yes, she's a homeless person. You'd never guess, would you, to look at her?"

"Yeah," says Hank, "I couldn't believe it when I saw her get that grocery cart."

"Doris isn't playing with a full deck, but I love her dearly. She started coming here a year ago, asking for a free cup of coffee, and over time I just sort of added items. Sometimes, after she has left, I'll find that she has left me a payment—in acorns or some such thing."

"Sad."

"Yes. Some other merchants and I tried to get her help—you know, a social worker and stuff like that—but she won't agree to anything. What can you do? She has the right to refuse." The waitress shakes her head and moves on to clear off other tables.

Hank scoops up my water bowl, tosses leftover water in the bushes, and we're off. Before long, we have left the freeway and are treated to the rolling countryside of Route 128 with its lush vineyards and scattered ranches. This is a new world for me, one in which I yearn to run free. Route 128 ends at the coast and now it's another complete change of scenery. We pass Albion and Little River and then I see it up ahead— Mendocino, with its white church spire and Victorian buildings announcing that this is a special, quaint village apart from the usual seaside community.

Hank stops the car at the edge of the town to consult a map that Stu gave him. Sarah's parents live on the other side of Mendocino, just off the main road. We find the place easily—a simple rectangular house with window boxes and an outbuilding at the rear. The window boxes hold only dirt.

Jack Schuler opens the door before Hank has a chance to knock. Jack is a weary looking old guy, his shoulders hunched over as if he carries a weight on his back. The blue eyes are kind, and they crinkle at the sight of Hank.

"I'm so glad to see you, Hank. This visit means a lot to me." He shakes Hank's hand. "Come on in."

"Do you mind if my dog comes, too? He can stay in the car if you prefer."

"Of course he can come in. What's his name?" Hank bends over to give me a scratch.

"Sam. He's a good dog." My chest swells with pride.

We enter a large living room with a kitchen/dining area sectioned off by a counter. In a chair by the window sits a frail wrinkled woman with a bleached-out face. She looks our way, but there is no other acknowledgment of our presence.

"You remember Emma," says Jack. "Em, this is Hank Arrowby, Sarah's neighbor. You met him a couple times when we visited Stu and Sarah." He leads Hank, who is looking a little taken aback, closer to Sarah's mother. Emma stares out the window.

Jack says, "It's pointless, I suppose, but I still act as if she understands everything." He motions to a chair. "Sit here, Hank. I know you have a lot to tell me." His eyes fill with tears. "I dread hearing it and yet at the same time I need to hear it—all of it. The detectives have talked with me, but it's the details I want. Stuart can't seem to get the words out."

"I know." Hank's eyes aren't too dry themselves. "That's why he wanted me to see you."

Hank launches into the story, starting at the beginning when he last saw Sarah. Occasionally, Jack interrupts with a question. After awhile I lose interest and walk around the room, sniffing objects. Jack's high top rubber boots sit near the front door. The odors are intoxicating: I recognize opossum and a faint odor of skunk; something strange and exciting, possibly coyote; two cat odors and a female dog. I sniff so vigorously that I'm nearly dizzy. I stagger away to check out an umbrella stand nearby and then I head for the far side of the room where Jack has thrown a sweater on a chair near a small bookcase. The sweater lacks the interest of the boots.

I end up at Emma's chair where I sit, looking at her. Emma turns her head to stare at me. There is no light in the eyes and a bit of saliva drools from her lower lip. Surprising me, she lifts a hand toward my head, a hint of a smile parting her lips. I edge closer and the hand plops on my nose like a dead thing.

"Omigod, will you look at that," Jack exclaims. "She's trying to pet your dog. That's the first time she's shown interest in anything, and I mean anything, for months. I can't believe it."

"Maybe you should get a dog," says Hank.

The dead hand falls from my head and the tiny smile fades away, leaving emptiness in its place.

"Maybe I should." Jack's voice trails off, but he rouses himself and sits up straighter. "Tell me, Hank, do you have any theories about who could have murdered Sarah? The cops are being so tight-lipped. You don't think it could be Stuart, do you?"

"Stu? Nah. They had a great marriage. Besides, I know Stu; he's not capable of murder. Anyway, remember that Sarah was seen driving off alone that day."

"You think it was some stranger? A random act of violence?"

"I dunno, Jack. I have my suspicions, one guy in particular, but I can't go around accusing people of murder when there is zero evidence."

"Are you thinking of that strange man on your street?"

"I'm more concerned about the man Sarah had an affair with."

"I could tell from your expression when you described him that you don't have much use for him." Jack shakes his head. "You know, I still can't get it through my skull that Sarah had an affair. So unlike her. As you say, she was going through a difficult time then. Emma and I never knew. If only we could have helped her."

"You couldn't have done anything, Jack. It was something she had to work out for herself. And she had Miriam, you know, so she wasn't without support. It's just unfortunate that Huddleston was the guy involved."

"Huddleston?"

"The bastard I'm suspicious about."

"You think he murdered her?"

"I don't know what I think anymore."

Hank sits stiffly erect, his mouth open in surprise. "I just thought of something! His first ex-wife lives in Mendocino. I'd completely forgotten about her. I should drop in on her. Could I see your phone book, Jack?"

While Jack searches for it, I wander around the room. Pictures of Sarah abound: Sarah as a preschooler riding a tricycle; Sarah in a graduation gown; Sarah on horseback; Sarah and Stu on their wedding day; Sarah's professional portrait, the same picture I had seen at her house. I walk past Sarah's mother and she doesn't look at me.

Hank pores over the phone book. "I wonder if she kept her married name, he mutters to himself. "Here it is. I'm in luck." He writes down the address.

Jack offers him a drink, but Hank declines. I think he's eager to see Huddleston's ex-wife and I know it's difficult for him to talk to Jack about Sarah.

"We'd better go," he says.

"You've helped me, Hank. I needed to know the details. And now I'm just waiting for Stuart to tell me when the memorial service will be."

"You seem to be bearing up. You already have so much to deal with, I don't know how you can handle it."

Jack seems to shrink into himself. "It hasn't hit me yet. Maybe when I'm there for the service. When I'm at the house and she isn't there. You know?"

"I know." The two men embrace and Hank turns to me, tears in his eyes. "C'mon, Sam, we have business to attend to."

In the car Hank consults his map, muttering to himself. We return to Mendocino proper, where he makes several wrong turns trying to find the house, but eventually we end up in front of the right place—a tiny brown-shingled home with blue shutters and a bright yellow front door. This owner is not afraid of color.

Walking up the gravel path to the entrance, I get an overpowering whiff of rosemary. The little front yard is crowded with herbs of all kinds and I wonder if the owner might give Hank some of these aromatic beauties for our kitchen. I expect Hank to stop and admire the garden; instead, he strides purposefully to the door and knocks.

"Coming." A feminine voice calls from the interior.

When the door is at last swung open, it reveals a sight even more colorful than the outside of the house. The sharp-faced woman with black hair pulled into a ponytail is wearing overalls layered with more paint colors than I thought could exist. Parts of the clothing are so thick with paint, I bet the overalls stand up all by themselves when the lady takes them off.

"Patti ?" says Hank. "It's Hank Arrowby. Remember me?"

"Hank! Of course. Come in, come in." Patti opens the door.

"Is it all right if my dog comes inside?"

"Sure, but I must warn you: I have two cats."

Cats?

Hank reaches down to give me a pat. "Sam is okay with cats. I'll have him stay close to me."

Patti laughs and motions for us to come inside. "It's not the cats you need to worry about. They can more than take care of themselves, believe me. I just don't want them to hurt your dog."

I am insulted.

Hank has me heel as we enter a room that is straight out of a jungle. Plants are everywhere: on tables; on plant stands; hanging from the ceiling. A large fern sits atop a chest of drawers straight in front of us, and lounging next to the plant is a gray-and-white mountain of fur.

Patti points to it. "That's Gordo. He's a Maine coon cat."

Gordo opens his eyes and gives me a disdainful stare. I can only hope that he stays on top of the dresser. I swear that cat is bigger than I am.

"I finished painting a few minutes ago," says Patti, "and I just need to get out of these overalls. Come see my studio."

She leads us to an adjoining room where we are met by another feline. This one is a calico, smaller and nastier than Gordo. It flattens its ears and hisses ferociously at me, daring me to take one more step. I freeze.

"Now, now, Princess, be nice." Turning to Hank, Patti says, "I call her Princess because she thinks she is one."

The cat opens her mouth and hisses again, louder this time. Princess lacks the manners of royalty.

Hank laughs, which I feel is inconsiderate of him, and places himself between Princess and me. "I'll protect you, Sam," he says.

I give a little "grrr" and we pass by the angry mound of fur.

While Patti removes her overalls, Hank and I gaze around the room at the oversized canvases propped against the walls. Bright colors pop out at us and abstract shapes jumbled together almost make me dizzy. I thought Brick's collages were weird, but this stuff is mind-boggling. I sneak a look at Hank and his mouth is open.

"Wow," he says. "You think big, don't you?"

Patti chuckles. "I'm glad you didn't say my painting is 'free'. So many people tell me that and I'm beginning to think what they really mean is 'out of control'." She turns and gestures toward a canvas behind us. The painting is huge, half the size of the wall on which it leans. The upper left of the canvas reminds me of the sun, because of the intense shades of red and yellow. The colors streak into the rest of the painting, merging with blurred shapes that could be anything—human or otherwise.

"This is my current baby—or nightmare—I'm not sure which. One minute I love it and the next minute I want to gesso over the whole thing."

"Why?" says Hank. "I like it."

It's not like Hank to lie. How can he like such wild stuff?

"Really?"

"Really. It's so free." They both laugh.

"How about a beer?" Patti says. "Then you can tell me what brings you to Mendocino."

"A beer would be fine. Thanks."

Princess is nowhere to be seen as we move on to the kitchen. I hope she stays hidden. Patti plunks two cold beer bottles on the small wooden table and pushes a bottle opener toward Hank.

"Would Sammy like some water?" she says.

I just wish some day somebody would offer me a beer, too. Why is it always just water?

"Sure, nice of you to think of him. I have his bowl in the car." Hank starts to rise, but Patti stops him.

"Don't bother. I'll use the cats' water bowl."

What?

Patti puts a ridiculous bowl in front of me. It's pink and decorated with stupid cat faces. Smells like a cat, too. I want to upchuck, but I'm so thirsty I force myself to drink out of it.

"So," Patti says, "tell me why you're here."

"I'm up here doing a favor for a friend, and when I remembered you live here I thought it would be a good opportunity to talk to you about Hud."

Patti's eyes widen. "Windsor?"

"I forgot. You always called him by his real first name."

"That, or 'Windy' during the early years when life was good. But we've been divorced a long time. I have no idea what he's doing now."

"That's not it. I want to ask you what he was like when you were living with him."

"Well, you worked closely with him fighting fires. You know what he was like."

Hank shakes his head. "What I mean is, I want to know from a woman's point of view. Just how dangerous was he?"

"Dangerous?"

"I know his second wife got a restraining order on him. Do you think Hud is capable of murder?"

"Murder?" Patti almost chokes on her beer. "What on earth are you talking about? Hank, you'd better start from the beginning."

Hank takes a long pull from the bottle. "I'm giving you the short version. My next door neighbor and friend, Sarah Fetzler, was murdered weeks ago. She was last seen driving away from the house. Her body was discovered on Tuesday in the mountains. She had no enemies that anyone is aware of and her marriage was sound. But we found out that she had an affair with Hud three years ago. Nobody except her business partner—she's a therapist—knew about it."

Patti blows out her breath in a dismissive way. "That hardly makes Windsor a murder suspect. And her marriage couldn't have been very sound if she had an affair. They oughta check out the husband."

"You'd have to know the couple to understand how compatible they are...were. Three years ago Sarah had a miscarriage, and there had been several before that. Miriam, her partner, says she was at a very vulnerable point and that the affair was meaningless. As for Stuart, Sarah's husband, he's been a wreck ever since she first went missing."

"This still doesn't make Windsor a murder suspect."

"Yesterday I saw him leaving the road where Sarah's body was found. I followed him to Santa Cruz. He met some guy on West Cliff Drive and handed him something. Not long after that he drove to his home in the mountains."

"You've been reading too many mysteries. There could be an innocent explanation."

"Maybe. Maybe not. He's a guy with a temper, that I know. So I'm asking you again: do you think he's capable of murder?"

For a moment Patti stares at Hank as if he's a lunatic, then drops her gaze and shakes her head. "I doubt it. Of course, who can say what another person is capable of. But murder? He did have a terrible temper, which is one of the reasons I divorced him. When he got mad at me he threw things at the wall. But if Windsor were to murder anyone it would have to be a case of temporary insanity. I was never afraid of him."

"I guess that answers my question."

Patti smiles and pats Hank on the hand. "Don't look so disappointed. You aren't really trying to play detective, are you?"

Hank gives her a weak smile in return and doesn't answer her.

"Well!" Patti pops up and beams at him. "Enough morbid talk. Why don't you stay for dinner?"

Oh, please, Hank, don't say yes. I'm not eating with cats.

"No, thanks," says Hank. "I just wanted to ask you about Hud. Sam and I will be on our way."

"Nonsense. You have to have dinner, and why pay for a meal when you can get one for free? I'll throw together some goulash and you can leave right after you eat, if you want to. I'd love the company, really I would."

"But..."

"No buts. Do you want wine or beer with your meal?"

"Beer is fine, thanks," says Hank, apparently unable to muster any more resistance.

"What about your dog? Will he eat cat food?"

Now there's a thought. I look at Hank, who is pushing away from the table and shaking his head. "I have his dog food in the car," he says.

I accompany him outside to the VW and watch him scoop up my dinner into the dog dish. He also gets my water bowl, for which I'm grateful. At least I won't have to look at dumb pink kitties while I drink.

Re-entering the house, we come face to face with Gordo, who has abandoned his spot atop the chest of drawers and is now on the floor, blocking our way. This is not a cat; it's a mountain lion with long hair. The mountain lion is not about to relinquish his space, and when we try to pass, he gives two quick swipes at my face with his paw, claws extended.

"Whoa, there," says Hank, shoving Gordo with his leg. Gordo's response is to snarl and hiss.

"Gordo!" yells Patti from the kitchen. "Dinner time!"

Gordo and the Princess must understand the word "dinner", because they both make a beeline for the kitchen. While they noisily slurp up food from their twin pink dishes, I eat my dinner as far away from them as Hank can put my bowls.

Patti's goulash concoction appears to be chiefly hamburger and macaroni mixed with tomato soup. When she sets it in front of Hank, he looks a trifle dubious, but Patti doesn't seem to notice.

They make small talk, exchanging personal histories covering the years since they last saw each other. Whether it's because of the two additional beers or simply Hank's company, I can't say, but Patti becomes more and more animated and her body language more suggestive. Twice she brushes against him when she gets refills for the table. Reaching for the saltshaker, she makes sure her cleavage is at his eye level.

"Hank, why don't you stay the night?" she asks. "Surely you're not going to drive all the way back to San Jose at this hour?"

Hank swallows hard. "I have a reservation at that motel with the little cabins. Thanks just the same."

"Oh, come on. Save your money." Patti gives him a smile dripping with promise of pleasures not provided at the motel.

Hank stands up abruptly. "Nope. Sorry. Motel's already paid for."

Now that I know is a lie. And am I glad.

Thanks a lot for the meal, Patti," Hank says, grabbing my dinner bowls. He holds the bowls in front of his stomach as we say our good-byes, probably to keep Patti at bay in case she gets any ideas about kissing him.

We hurry to the car and Hank wastes no time getting out of there. The place is full of predators.

Friday night, back in the safety of our home, Hank calls Ann Wonderful to tell her about our trip to Mendocino. He leaves out the part about Patti.

"Tommorow? I'm sorry, Annie, I have some work I need to do on the house. How about coming Sunday morning and staying over? You don't need to be at the gallery until Tuesday, anyway."

They chat a little longer and then Hank hangs up, all smiles. I'm so disgusted that I go to bed early, right after dinner. What's worse, Ann Schaefer appears in my dream. She has a monstrous cat on a leash and the two of them chase me for miles. I wake myself up, whimpering.

CHAPTER 16

Hank still wants to visit the spot where Sarah's body was found. The next day we're back in the VW. As much as I enjoy a ride in the car, I hope, in a way, that he'll once again get deflected from his goal, because I'm uneasy about going to a crime scene. My wish is denied. The ride up twisting Highway 9 is uneventful and there is no traffic on Skyline. We have the top of the mountain to ourselves.

I wonder what it would be like to live here. I know mountain living is not easy, because winter storms cause electric outages, too much rain can trigger mudslides, and in summer there is a fire danger. If Hank were cooking dinner and he discovered he was missing an ingredient, there would be no last minute running to the grocery store. But I would love it. If we had a home right here off Skyline, I could run leash-free and explore the scents of wild animals like mountain lions, skunks, and coyotes. I'm sorry Hank is a flatlander, the mountain folks' term for people who live in Santa Clara Valley.

Hank finds the road as Pete described it—between a huge boulder and a redwood tree that once was struck by lightning. It's a shaded dirt road riddled with potholes, causing me to bounce around in the back seat. Sort of a poor man's carnival ride.

"Hang on Sammy," says Hank.

About a mile into the place Hank stops at a small turnout. "Pete said this was the spot. Her body was found in the ravine near here."

It's a heavily forested area, the large fir trees blocking out the sun, but here and there are open spots such as the one we're in now. To our right is a steep ravine and Hank wants a closer look. We get out of the car and walk a short distance to the edge. My nose is assaulted with overlapping odors—clean fresh smells of young leaves, rotting vegetation, damp soil, and some scents I can't identify.

Nature has sent rocks and boulders crashing into the trees below; unfortunately, man has chosen to pitch his own discards into the ravine. A rusted green shell of a car, rear end up, is wedged part way under a fallen pine. Half a dozen tires lie scattered about and I see what looks like boards and a wheel from an ancient wagon. I imagine Sarah's body being heaved over the edge like so much garbage. I'm sick to my stomach. Hank must feel the same, because he turns away and his face is the color of cornstarch.

We're almost back into the car when I spot it—a rabbit scooting down the road. I can't help myself. Some instincts are so deeply imbedded they are beyond our control and, true to my genes, I take off after that son-of-a-gun. Hank is yelling at me, but nothing can stop me now.

I didn't know rabbits could run so fast. This one veers into the woods and I go crashing after him, scraping my snout on brambles and lurching into broken branches that seem to be aiming themselves directly at my sides.

The rabbit vanishes. I'm too tired to bother tracking his scent and I simply stand there panting as I've never panted in my life. When at last my breathing has calmed, a new and unpleasant awareness creeps over me. I am lost.

Any dog worth its salt should be able to retrace its steps by scent alone, but I'm too confused. There are too many unfamiliar odors bombarding my nostrils. If only I could hear Hank's voice. I prick up my ears. There is something—something human, but it's not Hank.

I pick my way through the woods, homing in on the sounds, until I find myself on a narrow dirt road, more like a wide path than a road, and a hundred feet away sits a large ramshackle cabin and two out buildings. Jugs, boxes and tools litter the yard. A beat-up orange pickup is parked off to the side. Two men, a blond one with a bodybuilder's physique and the other tall and skinny with a fu-manchu moustache, lean against the truck.

"I'll be damned," says the blond guy. "Look what's coming."

Fu-manchu turns around. "Hey, pooch, how'd you get here?" His voice is high and brittle. I don't like it. I'm hopeful, though, so I close in on the men.

Loud, deep barks startle me and my hairs stand on end at the sight of two powerful Rottweilers barreling toward us.

"Rocky! Stay!" yells Blondie.

Both dogs screech to a halt, tongues hanging out, tail stubs wagging.

"Aw, let 'em sniff. They don't get to have visitors very often," says Fu-manchu, and he laughs.

Rocky and his female circle me, sniffing my privates for a minute, then wander off. They give no signals of wanting to play, but they show no aggression, either. Apparently they consider me insignificant. Irrational as it may be, I'm insulted.

"Let's see the tags." Blondie pulls me roughly by the collar. "San Jose area code. Says his name is Sammy,"

Fu-manchu picks at his moustache. "Wearing tags and well fed. He wasn't dumped and hasn't been long in the woods. That means an owner somewhere. Shit."

Blondie yells, "Marnie! C'mere!"

A screen door slams and a young woman in cut-offs and a dirty tank top approaches us. She's as skinny as Fu-manchu with long brown hair that she intermittently tucks behind her ears. A twitchy sort of person. I'm surprised to find myself actually longing for Ann Schaefer.

"Take this dog inside," says Blondie.

"What the hell am I supposed to do with him? I'm busy."

"Just keep him inside. We'll get rid of him later."

Get rid of him? What are they going to do to me? I don't want to die.

The Marnie woman pulls on my collar, but I dig in my heels. If she loosens her grip I'll take off for the woods.

"Aw, fuck," says Fu-manchu. "Here comes trouble."

Far down the road, limping rapidly toward us, is Hank. I yearn to run to him, but Marnie has a firm grip.

"You call that trouble?" says Blondie. "The guy can't even run. Hell, he can hardly walk."

"You never know. Remember the hikers who turned out to be narcs."

"You're getting paranoid, Carl," says Marnie.

"Shut up."

Marnie gives him the finger with her free hand, but Carl Fu-manchu doesn't notice.

Hank waves his cane at us. "That's my dog," he yells. "Sammy, come."

I strain, but Marnie holds tight. "Why not let the dog go?" she says.

"Nobody asked you, woman. Here, I'll hold him for you. You get the gun."

Carl yanks me away from Marnie who quickly returns with a shotgun that must have been just inside the cabin door. These people are not rational, I decide, and I'm afraid for Hank, who reaches us at last.

He is so out of breath, he can barely get the words out. "I said...that's...my dog."

Marnie has passed the gun to Blondie, but Hank acts as uninterested as if she had handed the guy a broom.

"Let go of him," says Hank.

"How do we know it's your dog?" says Blondie.

"Don't be ridiculous," Hank says. "Would I be running after him otherwise?"

Blondie smirks. "You call that running?" Carl snickers and color creeps up Hank's face.

"Maybe the dog was running away from you," says Blondie. "Maybe we should keep him for his own safety." The hairs on my back stand up.

"Look," says Hank, "I don't want any trouble. I just want my dog back."

"Prove he's your dog. What's his name?"

"Sam."

"That's not what the tag says."

"Of course that's what it says." Hank's eyes brighten with anger and his fists are clenched.

"Nope. His name is Sammy." Blondie shifts the shotgun to his other side.

Hank stands immobile, his eyes on the gun, and for what seems like a very long time we all are motionless, silent, like performers in a theatrical tableau.

Carl brings us to life. "Fuck, take the dog. This is a waste of my fucking time." He releases my collar, shoves me toward Hank, and stomps off, Marnie following.

Blondie isn't finished. He hoists his gun, finger on the trigger, and his eyes narrow. "We don't like trespassers," he says. The words are cold, hard, deliberate—each one a bullet.

Hank wisely keeps his mouth shut. Meanwhile, I'm calculating whether I could be fast enough to bite Blondie on the leg before he pulled the trigger. I'm saved from making a tragic error when Blondie waves the shotgun toward the road. "Get the fuck outta here," he says.

Hank and I are only too eager to comply. "Heel," says Hank, and we walk away toward safety and a saner world.

At home, Hank gets Detective Holcomb on the phone once again. He delivers a blow-by-blow of our terrifying experience on the mountain, his voice rising and the words coming faster the further he gets into the story. By the end of it I'm scared all over again. The detective's response must not be the one that Hank is anticipating, because his face sags when he hangs up. "Why do I bother?" he says.

Pete and Hank sit on our patio with their feet propped up on extra chairs, nursing beers and watching the clouds turn a luscious pink in the western sky. Trish, Pete's wife, must have pried him away from his model trains and made him do yard work, because there are grass stains on his knees and dirt is embedded in the creases of his fingers. I think he may have had a harder day in his back yard than on police patrol.

"Sunset in Santa Cruz must be spectacular tonight," says Pete.

"Yeah," says Hank. "I like living close to the mountains but they do block the sunsets."

Pete shifts his weight and takes another pull on his beer. "Speaking of Santa Cruz, you ought to think twice about following Windsor Huddleston all over the map. He could get you for harassment."

"Naw. He never saw me."

"How do you know? Just because he didn't acknowledge you doesn't mean he didn't see you. He knows your vehicle. Hank, you're letting your dislike for him cloud your judgment."

"Maybe. And then there's Brick. I forgot to tell you. On the way home from Santa Cruz I got asked by his mother to check some vase she had bought. I discovered that Brick had Sarah's butterfly pin in a new collage of his. I reported it to Lieutenant Holcomb, but he was so noncommittal I'm not sure whether he bothered following up on that."

Pete suppresses a smile. "Don't kid yourself. They follow up on everything. He can't let on what he's doing, that's all."

"I suppose. When I called him about today's little excursion he wanted all the details, then he warned me to stay away, and after that he clammed up."

"I'm afraid to ask. What little excursion was this?"

I stop scratching my ear and watch Pete's face as Hank recounts our ordeal of the morning., Pete plunks down his beer and juts out his lower lip. The relaxed features of Hank's old friend transform into the steel edged ones of a seasoned cop. His black face somehow darkens even more, if that's possible.

"What the hell do you think you're doing, Hank? Are you nuts? You want to get yourself killed? That's a nasty bunch up there."

"You know about them?"

"Sure. It's Sheriffs territory, but San Jose PD got involved a couple of times. There are fifteen or twenty people in that group—some kind of gothic cult or whatever. They've been busted in the past for cooking meth." Pete leans forward to slap a beefy hand on Hank's knee. "Hank. Listen to me, man. You have to stop this amateur sleuthing. It'll get you nowhere and you'll just end up making a total ass of yourself."

"I'm so damn frustrated," says Hank, leaning back in his chair and closing his eyes. "Knowing Sarah's killer is out there, walking around free—I can't tell you how angry that makes me."

"I know. Believe me, I know."

"As for Stu, it's even worse for him. The guy's a wreck."

A fly zips by my nose and I snap at him, but miss. Damn bugs. Not caring to hear any more of the conversation, I doze off. I dream I'm chasing a rabbit down our street and I almost catch him, but he runs into the Hoyt's house. There he turns into Crabby Crawford who points a shotgun at me. I turn tail and try to run away, but my legs are heavy and I can only move in slow motion. I wake up to find Hank and Pete looking at me and laughing.

It's not funny.

CHAPTER 17

Surely this has been the most eventful week of my life. Too eventful. I'm ready for a relaxing Sunday doing nothing more stressful than lying around in the shade watching ants on parade.

It's not to be. Curly-head Cutie arrives mid-morning, suitcase in hand and a glittering smile plastered on her face. She and Hank greet each other with way too much enthusiasm.

Ann hasn't been in the house more than five minutes when the doorbell rings. It's Stu, looking as if he has shrunk in size. Is it possible that stress can make a person wither away?

"Oh, I'm sorry," he says, when Hank opens the door. "I didn't realize you had company." He turns to leave, but Hank stops him.

"Come meet Ann," he says.

Stu and Ann are introduced, there is commiseration about the awful state of affairs, and I hope Stu will remain with us, but his visit is short.

"I need help," he says. "The coroner's office returned Sarah's remains and they're being cremated. I need to plan a memorial service. Miriam Weinberg has agreed to come over this afternoon around two o'clock and your input would be appreciated as well. There are photographs to look through, music to be decided, that sort of thing. The minister will come, too. I want to get this over with as soon as possible, so I'm looking at next weekend for the service. It'll be in the chapel at the mortuary."

"Sure, Stu. I'll be there." Hank's voice shows no trace of disappointment, but I have no doubt he had far more pleasurable plans in mind for the afternoon.

"I suppose there will have to be a reception," Stu says.

"Of course. Sarah knew a lot of people and everybody loved her. They will want to speak to you, you know."

"I don't think I can stand it, Hank."

"Look, why don't we have the reception here? That way, if you feel like taking a break, you can just pop over to your house for awhile."

"And I'd be happy to help with that," Ann pipes up in her chirpy little voice.

Something tells me she doesn't handle the topic of death easily. Her cheeriness contrasts starkly with Stu's gloom.

Stu expresses his gratitude and shuffles off.

Hank suggests a walk through the neighborhood, sort of an orientation stroll for Ann and exercise for me, which is a great idea, provided he doesn't hand her the leash. When Hank opens the front door, the sun smacks us like a strobe light, portending another hot day. Hank says he doesn't remember a heat wave ever lasting as long as this one. Luckily, our street boasts numerous sycamore trees, so periodically we move through shade.

"We're being watched, of course," says Hank, inclining his head toward Crabby's house.

We saunter down the street and Hank points out the Foyt home. "This is where Brick lives," he says. "Real name is Arthur. Very odd fellow who lives with his elderly mother. He creates collages and recently I discovered he had a piece of Sarah's jewelry in one of them."

Ann stops short and her red curls take a bounce. "You think he could have murdered Sarah? This doesn't look like a murderer's house, does it? It's so cutesy."

Now that I'm taking time to analyze the place, I see what she means. The house is painted a barn red and the white shutters have scalloped edges. A low white picket fence encircles the yard, which contains rose bushes and a fountain in the center. On the edge of the fountain sits a concrete squirrel.

Hank chuckles. "I never thought about it, but you're right. It is cutesy. You're making me see my neighborhood with new eyes, Annie."

"It's a nice area," says Ann, as we continue our stroll. "Even though it's an older development, people keep up their yards and pay attention to their homes. It looks like a good neighborhood to bring up children."

Across the street Anthony Meissner and his friends are practicing basketball lay-ups in his driveway. Anthony looks as if he's grown two inches every time I see him, and his brown hair changes color like a chameleon. Last week it was orange and this week it has a purple stripe down the center. After we have continued to the corner, crossed the street and returned, passing in front of the Meissner's, Hank calls a greeting to Anthony. One of the boys turns to stare, but Anthony pays no attention.

"Hi, Anthony," Hank says again.

Anthony dribbles the ball and leaps high to dunk it through the hoop. "Hi," he grunts, but he doesn't look at us.

"Teenagers," mutters Hank, and we move on.

Bud Manolo, the lovable slob who lives next door to Crabby, is sitting out front of his house in a tattered lawn chair, writing on a tablet. He hefts himself out of the chair to move a hose, dropping the tablet in the process. We move in for introductions and Bud runs a hand through his hair, fumbles with a button on his Hawaiian shirt, and rubs both hands on his pants, all in a fruitless attempt to improve his appearance for Ann.

"Pleased to meetcha," he says, hitching up his pants.

"You dropped this," says Hank, and picks up the tablet, raising his eyebrows when he sees the writing.

"Yeah, yeah." Bud grabs the tablet from him. "Don't tell anybody I write poetry, okay?"

"Afraid it'll spoil your image?" Hank is grinning.

"Something like that."

We take our leave of Bud and I'm surprised that Hank steers us back across the street instead of passing Crabby's house.

"It's too hot," he says to Ann. "Let's go back inside."

In the coolness of our living room, Hank and Ann relax with drinks of ice water and I try to refrigerate my belly by stretching out on the hardwood floor.

The phone rings and Hank reaches for the portable.

"Hi, Pete. What's up?"

Ann smiles at the name. Pete dropped in one time when Hank and Ann were first dating and Hank was cooking dinner for her. He flopped into a chair, making himself at home like he usually does, but that time Hank didn't seem to appreciate it. Pete told stories about his and Hank's escapades when they were kids, and Ann laughed until tears streamed down her face. After Pete had left, Ann told Hank how much she liked his friend. I was wishing she'd leave Hank for him, but Pete was already married.

"No," says Hank to Pete. "It was the woman who brought the shotgun out. They called her Marnie." Pause. "Carl was the name of the skinny guy." Pause. "No, those were the only names I heard." Pause. "Sure, Pete. So long."

Hank hangs up and avoids looking at Ann, whose face is one big question mark.

"Shotgun?" she says. "Hank, what have you been up to?"

Hank manages a weak smile and gives her a toned-down version of yesterday's experience on Skyline. At the end of his story he holds his hands out, palms upward.

"The only reason I didn't tell you my real plans for yesterday was because I didn't want to upset you. I knew you didn't think I should go to the crime scene. Of course, I had no idea I'd be running into those nut cases up there."

In a quiet voice, each of her words spoken slowly and distinctly, Ann says, "You lied to me."

"I was only trying not to worry you, honey. It's okay."

"You don't get it. You *lied* to me."

"But..."

"This is not okay." Anne carefully places her glass on a coaster and leans forward, her body as tense as a stretched bungee cord. "I won't have it!"

"Calm down. All I did was..."

"What do you mean, *calm down*?" Ann's face is as red as her curls and the bungee cord lets go. She bounds out of the chair in a single motion. "You lied! *Lied*! I had a fiancé who did nothing but lie, remember? I will not tolerate lying! I want nothing to do with a person who lies. I thought you were different." Her voice breaks on the last word and her eyes glisten.

By now I'm sitting upright and enjoying the spectacle.

"Annie, please." Hank leaps from his chair and attempts to pull Ann into his arms, but she wriggles away from him.

"Don't touch me."

"Oh, come on, Ann. You're overreacting."

"Overreacting? Well, excuse me for being upset because I've been lied to."

"It wasn't really lying. You're all worked up over nothing."

"Nothing? I've got news for you. To me it's something"

"What is the matter with you?" Hank looks genuinely perplexed.

"With me? With you, more like it. I'm out of here."

"Fine. Go." Hank retreats to his chair.

I'm both surprised and overjoyed that he doesn't try to stop her. Now Hank and I can have our old relationship back. After Ann stomps out of the house, I snuggle up to him and lay my head on his leg. Every muscle on his face is sagging. I stuff my muzzle into his limp hand, knowing that if he strokes my head he'll feel better, but he shoves me away. Rebuffed, I slink off to my blanket in the corner.

In the afternoon, I am left on my own while Hank goes next door to meet with Miriam and Stu to plan the memorial service. His mood is as morose when he returns as when he left. What a depressing day this has turned into.

Hours later, as Hank is readying for bed, the phone rings and it's Her Nibs. Although I hear only one side of the conversation, I can tell that she's all apologies, and Hank is full of the same. He tells her about the plans for the memorial service and then arranges to meet Ann tomorrow for dinner and a movie.

Damn!

CHAPTER 18

Hank wouldn't take me to Sarah's memorial service and I think it's unfair. The service is being held in some chapel and they don't serve food in a chapel, so why shouldn't I be allowed in? I loved her as much as anybody else did, after all, and I miss her terribly. I miss the gentleness of her hand when she stroked me, the way she would tilt back her head and laugh when I tore into the kitchen at the sound of a meat package being opened, the smile that lit up her face when she saw Hank and me.

Just to show my indignation at being left out, I leap onto the forbidden chair by the living room window and peer out at the street. Everyone is at the service, even Mrs. Crawford. It seems strange not to see her rocking in her porch chair. The view is so boring that I prepare to jump down, when a movement catches my eye. It's Brick Foyt, walking slowly past our house. The man not only is built like a brick, he walks like a brick—lurching stiff-legged side to side. He stops to look up and down the street, then continues to the front of the Fetzler's. I think he must be talking to himself, because his mouth is working. He stands there for several minutes, just looking at the place and talking. As he walks back past our house he sees me staring out the window and stops. A little shiver travels the length of my spine. I wonder if Hank remembered to lock the door. To my surprise, Brick laughs and lurches back toward his house.

As he passes from my sight, it occurs to me that I could follow him, provided our side gate is not latched. I race through the house, out the doggie door in the kitchen, and around to the narrow yard by the studio. I'm in luck. Hank has been careless; the gate latch is not secure.

With my body low to the ground, I stuff my nose under the gate and back up, pulling the gate to open it. The boards are rough and I know my nose is scraped, but I'm determined to see what that crazy man is up to. The gate swings open just wide enough to allow me to squeeze through.

I'm in time to spot Brick walking toward the back of his house. The Hoyts don't have a regular gate at their side yard. Theirs is a fence with a swinging gate that goes back and forth in either direction and doesn't latch. It is high off the ground, too, leaving me room to pass through underneath.

Approaching the corner of the house cautiously, I peer around. Brick has reached his workshop, as he calls it—a long three-sided affair at the rear of the property, set atop a concrete slab. Boxes filled with god-knows-what line the shelves above his workbench, which is cluttered with tools. Wood pieces, picture frames, and metal strips lean against the right wall. A makeshift roof of wood boards and a blue tarp cover all.

I slink along the grass to a photinia bush where I can disappear in the shadows. Brick reaches into a box and pulls out a large shiny object. He giggles while he holds it up to the light and twirls it around his fingers. I wish I could be closer to see what it is. He sets it onto the workbench, picks up a hammer and, to my astonishment, smashes it to bits. This produces more giggling.

And the surprises aren't over yet. The gate swings open, admitting a matchstick-thin, twenty-something guy with geeky green hair that looks like a botched-up Mohawk.

"Hey, Brick," the stranger calls.

"Yo."

The two give each other high fives and I'm bowled over. Whoever would have thought that reclusive old Brick would have a friend?

Brick and Matchstick make an odd duo: one the match, the other the matchbox. In a moment of perversity I imagine them burning themselves up.

They hover together over the workbench, selecting broken bits from Brick's demolition and holding them up to the light for critical examination. Connoisseurs of the absurd.

Brick separates the pieces into two piles, one of which he dumps into a bag for Matchstick.

"Wanna beer?" he asks.

"Yeah, sure."

If Hank could see this he wouldn't believe it: Brick the host.

While Brick is in the house, Matchstick entertains himself rummaging through Brick's supplies. From a box at the end of the workbench he retrieves a battered toy car that he winds up and sets on the ground. To my alarm, it heads directly for my bush, bouncing and careening through the grass. I lie perfectly still, hoping my blackness blends into the shadows of the photinia.

Matchstick's long strides bring him so close that I am overpowered by his odors: a potent combination of fried chicken, beer, sweat, tobacco, and grease. With effort I refrain from poking my nose out to sniff what other scents he might be carrying.

"Stupid thing." Matchstick grabs the toy and tosses it into the box.

When Brick returns with the beers, the men plant themselves into plastic lawn chairs. I worry they might be there for so long that I won't get back to the house before Hank.

Matchstick takes a long pull on his bottle. "You sure nobody is gonna find it?"

"Quit worrying. It's too well hidden."

"I dunno. You never know. Somebody might just walk there."

"Will you cut it out? Nobody is going to go there. Nobody."

"What if there's an earthquake? The ground will heave up and there it'll be."

"Jesus Christ. I'm sorry I gave you a beer. You're driving me nuts."

"Aw, fuck." Matchstick gets up, beer in hand. "I'm leaving."

"Don't forget your stuff."

Matchstick grabs his bag of mysterious pieces and stomps past me, leaving tantalizing odors in his wake.

For a good fifteen minutes Brick slouches in his chair, finishing the beer. I'm itching to be out of here and home before Hank returns. I consider creeping away, close to the fence, staying in the shadows as much as possible, but I'm saved this risky attempt when Brick heaves himself up and plods to the workbench, his back toward me.

I move slowly, careful not to make any noise, then I race down the street to our side gate. Apparently, I've used up all my luck quotient for the day, because the gate is now securely latched. It must have closed hard behind me when I left and there is no other way to the back yard. I lie down resignedly on the front steps to await my fate.

Hank and Ann return before the others. I start to wag my tail, but at the sight of Hank's scowl my tail droops and I hang my head in shame.

"Sam! What are you doing outside?"

Fortunately for me, Hank and Ann are too pressed for time to bother with me and my indiscretions. They rush around, uncovering plates of hors d'oeuvres and getting cold drinks from the refrigerator. The house is soon filled with chattering people. I settle into a corner where I am able to watch and hear without getting in the way, thus avoiding being exiled to the studio.

Dogs have a point of view unknown to humans. We are experts on lower extremities. How a person handles his or her feet and legs discloses almost as much about the individual as the hands. For example, the legs of the man who has inched his way to my corner are restless; he stands first on one foot, then the other, and remains by himself. I take a sniff of the back of his legs and don't like what I smell. I spot Hank's legs approaching and they plant themselves in front of the man.

"What are you doing here?" Hank demands.

I look up in surprise to find that the restless legs belong to Windsor Huddleston.

"If you must know, I'm hoping to speak to Stuart. I assume he's going to be here?"

Hank ignores the question. "You've got a hell of a nerve showing your face. Stu has enough to deal with without putting up with your antics. Why don't you spare the man any more pain and get lost?"

There is a long moment of silence in which Hud stares at Hank, his eyes narrowing. "Just what are you playing at, Arrowby?"

"What do you mean?"

A pair of curvaceous legs in black stockings approaches, breaking the tension, and Huddleston moves away. I realize that the legs belong to Ann and I fault her for covering them up with baggy pants at other times. Female legs are far more interesting under skirts. If they only knew.

"Who is that man?" Ann asks.

"That, my dear, is the infamous Windsor Huddleston, renowned firefighter, notorious ladies' man, and general, all-around jerk."

"So you don't like him?" Crinkles have formed at Ann's eyes and she suppresses a smile.

"We need to make more coffee." Hank stomps off.

Since Hank doesn't appear to care that I am around, I move into the crowd, eavesdropping on snatches of conversation and hoping for dropped crumbs here and there.

"It was a lovely service, wasn't it? So like Sarah."

"Stu seems to be taking it really hard."

"....but what I don't understand...."

"These cream puffs are scrumptious."

"...and I hear the cops are going..."

It's all a bunch of blather, if you ask me. Why do people feel they have to eat because they've been to a funeral? Does something happen there to stimulate their appetites? Frankly, I wish they'd all go home.

I spot a pair of stubby legs with sensible shoes and I head in the opposite direction. If I get anywhere near Crabby Crawford she'll throw a fit and I don't want Hank upset at a time like this. As I move closer to the foyer, Stu enters quietly. Seeing me, he squats, scratches me under the ears, and presses his forehead on mine.

"Aw, Sammy, old boy, you're such a good dog."

My heart jumps and I lick him right on the face. I'd like to spend more time with him, but we're interrupted by Pete, who lays a hand on Stu's shoulder.

"Stu, it was a great service, a real tribute to Sarah."

"Thanks, Pete." Stu's eyes well up with tears.

A new voice bears down on us. "Stuart! It was a lovely service, just lovely." The voice owns legs that aren't as curvy as Ann's, but the black suit is first class.

"Thank you for coming, Vera," says Stu. "I'd like you to meet Pete Peters, one of San Jose's finest. Pete, this is Councilwoman Vera Escobar."

While pleasantries are exchanged, I observe the lady. No wonder Stu has enjoyed his meetings with her about the theater proposal. She's a stunner: light brown skin, eyes almost black, and a face perfectly sculpted either by God or a talented plastic surgeon. She puts a manicured hand on Stu's arm and pats him gently.

"I'm so sorry," she says. "I know it's about the hundredth time I've said it to you, but truly I feel so bad about what's happened. I wish I could do something for you."

"Thanks, but the best everyone can do is just carry on as normal and one of these days I'll catch up to the rest of you."

Hank spies us then, and escorts Stu into the living room where he continues to receive condolences and embraces. Miriam Weinberg is one of those who folds her arms around him and even kisses him on the cheek. She doesn't say a word, nor does she need to. Vera Escobar keeps a respectful distance, but doesn't stray far from Stu and she watches him intently, as if she's expecting him to pass out at any moment. Mrs. Foyt, Brick's mother, approaches Stu tentatively, bulldog jowls trembling. From my vantage point it looks as if Stu spends more time consoling her than vice versa.

As the commotion subsides, I look for Windsor Huddleston, curious about how he's going to handle this. He has remained at the edge of the crowd, twiddling an empty wine glass and shifting his weight from one foot to the other. When Stu at last is without someone hanging onto him, Huddleston comes forward. Stu's body stiffens.

"Before you say anything," says Huddleston, "I want to offer my apologies for my behavior that time at your house. I was out of line."

Stu, who must have been readying himself for a confrontation, appears to deflate at the unexpected apology. "I agree, you were."

"It wasn't just that I was angry because I'd been interviewed. I really cared for Sarah, and even though it was over between us a long time ago, it made me a little nuts to think something might have happened to her. You understand?"

Stu frowns and a muscle in his cheek twitches.

"I understand that you have some nerve expecting me to have any empathy for you. You have a lot of gall showing up here."

"Okay. I don't blame you. Forget it." Huddleston sets his half-empty wine glass on a table and exits the house.

Vera Escobar has been watching the exchange and now she positions herself at Stu's side. The manicured hand once again pats his arm.

"Who was that?" she asks.

"Nobody, believe me."

"You seem upset."

"I'm not upset." Stu pivots and strides out to the kitchen where Hank is refilling a plate with stuffed mushrooms. The scowl on the Escobar face mars its beauty and I search elsewhere for entertainment. Seeing Brick Foyt's mother in animated discussion with Mrs. Meissner, her neighbor down the street, I sidle up to Mrs. Foyt. Her jowls are shaking like jelly.

"It's discrimination!" she says. "They made Arthur go downtown to be interviewed and they kept him there for hours. Hours! I know Arthur sometimes acts a little odd, but just because he's different is no reason to think he's a killer. When he got home he went straight to his room and wouldn't even come out for dinner. He's hardly gone outdoors since. He refused to go to the memorial service, too, and I know he'd have been there, otherwise, because he really liked Sarah Fetzler."

"The detectives have been questioning a lot of people, not just Brick—I mean Arthur."

"See? You're as bad as the rest. You can't even call him by his Christian name." Mrs. Foyt gives a sniff and heads for the door.

"I'm sorry, I didn't mean..." Mrs. Meissner looks stricken and scans the room for her husband.

This reception seems to be bringing out the worst in people. At least it's not boring. Hearing the word "mailbox" I turn around and find myself behind Crabby Crawford, who has trapped some poor man in the corner.

"Don't you think it's strange?" she asks. "The vandalism stopped right around the time Sarah disappeared."

"I didn't notice."

"Neither did I, at first, but when I look back on it, I think Hank's mailbox was the last one. There must be a connection."

"Hmmm."

"And I've told those detectives about it, but they don't seem interested."

The man's mouth opens but he doesn't get a chance to speak.

"How can crimes be solved if police don't pay attention to what they're told?"

At that point Crabby takes a step backward and lands squarely on my left front paw. She may have a chicken face, but her body is a cow's. I can't help it; I yelp in pain. She whirls around and then recoils as if she has seen a monster. People nearby rush to my aid and I happily succumb to their soothing pats. Hank appears, but I wish he hadn't, because I don't want him to think I caused a commotion.

Crabby Crawford's face juts in front of Hank's. "There is a law," she sniffs, "about having dogs near food that's being served."

"I don't think that applies to the dog's home," says Hank, and he's smiling, thank God.

"Well, I never!" Crabby does a one-eighty and leaves in a huff.

The attrition rate at this affair is remarkable.

After soothing myself with a nap in the bedroom, I meander back to the living room and find that most of the guests have left. Only Hank, Ann, Miriam and Pete are left, sprawled on the furniture like marionettes without their strings. Even Ann has lost her usual enthusiasm.

"I should empty the dishwasher and put in another load," she says, but she doesn't move.

"Aw, leave it, honey," says Hank. "Just relax for awhile. Want some wine? Anybody?"

Pete and Ann shake their heads and Miriam raises the glass in her hand. "Gossum," she says. Miriam is sloshed.

"How come Sarah's father wasn't here?" asks Pete.

"A last minute problem," says Hank. "Poor guy. The lady who was to take care of Emma while Jack was gone got sick and it was too late for Jack to dredge up a replacement. Now Stu has to take the ashes to Mendocino for scattering in the ocean. He wants me to ride up with him in a couple days."

My ears perk up at this news. Surely Hank would never leave me at home alone for such a long time.

Hank takes a sip of his wine and stares into the glass. "So, Pete," he says, "what do you think?"

"About what? The trip to Mendocino?"

Hank sighs. "The case, funny man, the case. Heard anything?"

"They're being real tight-lipped. Sorry."

"Stu's getting paranoid about it. He's seeing deputies under every bush. Thinks they're watching his movements each time he leaves the house."

"Maybe they are. Face it, Hank, the husband is always a suspect."

"Thash ridiculush," says Miriam. "I've known Shtu longer than any of you, and there'sh no way, no way at all, that he coulda murdered Sharah."

"Believe me, Miriam," says Pete, "you never know what somebody's capable of. More often than not, it's a spouse or lover or ex—someone close to the victim."

"But not Shtu." Miriam's glass is tipping and her wine is dangerously close to spilling over.

"I know how you feel. I like Stu; I like him a lot. And I'm not saying I think he did it, but what I am saying is that you have to realize nothing is impossible when it comes to murder."

"I knew somebody who killed his wife," says Ann. All heads turn to look at her. Even I want to hear what she has to say—for the moment, anyway.

"It was in La Jolla, my hometown. My parents belonged to a couple of bridge groups, and one of the people was this lawyer, very respected guy, and he strangled his wife. It was after they got home from playing bridge at our house. My parents couldn't believe it."

"She probably trumped his ace," says Hank, and he and Pete guffaw. Ann and Miriam just stare at him.

"My parents didn't think it was funny," says Ann, her face almost as red as her curls.

Hank is still snickering at his own joke, which makes me hopeful that Miss Wonderful will get mad enough to leave—forever. Instead, she gets up, pours herself a glass of wine, and settles beside Miriam on the sofa.

Miriam says, "Pete, wha' about the other guys?"

"What guys?"

"Other shushpecs."

Hank can't help himself. "Sushpecs, Miriam?" he says, smirking. "Have some more wine."

Pete ignores Hank and answers Miriam seriously. "Don't worry, Miriam, they'll follow all leads. I know Detective Holcomb personally. He's a good guy, one of the best, and tenacious. If anyone can solve this case it's him.

"Thash good to know."

"What about that strange fellow, Brick somebody, who lives down the street?" asks Ann.

My ears have perked up at the mention of Brick and I'm frustrated that I have no ability to speak. If they only knew what I had seen today.

Pete turns toward Hank. "Is Brick a true artist? I know there's such a thing as found art."

"The only similarity between Brick's stuff and true found art is that he creates from discarded articles. He has no artistic talent. Some of his creations are pretty loony, not what anyone would buy."

Ann pipes up. "People probably thought Jackson Pollock's work was loony in the beginning."

"I still think Pollock's work is loony," says Hank. Do I detect some tension between him and Ann? I can only hope.

"Have you ever seen Brick interact with Sarah?" asks Pete.

"Sure. She was always very nice to him, always treated him like a normal person. He acted very shy and tongue-tied around her. I can't picture Brick murdering her. However, he does do some strange things. For instance, several weeks ago I saw him hanging around the Fetzler's fence, the one on the Branham Lane side."

"What was he doing?"

"I don't know. Just trying to see through the fence, I guess. It was after Sarah disappeared, and for all I know he thought he was looking for Sarah. Crabby saw him, too."

Pete grins. "That woman is a policeman's dream."

"Whenever I come over here I feel so self-conscious," says Ann, "because I know she's watching my every move."

"The one I'm worried about," says Hank, "is Windsor Huddleston. Hud. There's a guy I have no problem picturing committing murder."

"I don't blame you," says Pete. "But what he did to you doesn't make him a murderer. In fact, Hank, if Hud were found dead, you'd be an immediate suspect. Ever think of that?"

Hank just shrugs his shoulders, but Ann perks up. "What are you talking about?" she asks.

Hank sighs. "Windsor Huddleston is the guy I told you about. The one who filled my girlfriend with all kinds of crap about me, none of it true, but she believed him. Then he dated her and finally he dumped her like he's dumped so many others."

"But why would she have believed him in the first place? She must have been awfully gullible."

"You don't know Hud. Women can't get enough of him. Don't ask me to explain it. He's a great firefighter but when it comes to social interaction he's a piece of shit."

"Amen to that," says Miriam. "I'm with you, Hank. I find it very shuspicious that Sharah had an affair with him that she kept shecret and now she's dead." Miriam has finally drained her glass and she sets it down with a thud. "Oh, God, I'm drunk."

Pete stands up to stretch. "I need to get home," he says. "Trish left an hour ago." As Hank accompanies him to the door, Pete clamps a hand on Hank's shoulder. "It's okay, buddy. They'll find the killer."

Nobody looks too reassured at those words, though, and tears are spilling down Miriam's cheeks.

"Let's get you home," says Hank, pulling Miriam to her feet and hugging her tightly. "I'll bring your car over tomorrow."

I'm at Hank's side, ready to roll, but he tells me to stay. "You keep Annie company, old boy. I'll be back in half an hour, Ann."

"I'm sorry, Hank, but I need to leave, too." She gives Hank a hug and the three head out the door, paying no attention to me. What am I, dirt?

I stretch out on the living room floor, listening to the silence. It still seems impossible that Sarah was murdered. Sometimes I wonder why dogs ever attached themselves to the human race, these complicated beings who don't understand each other, who try so hard but end up hurting themselves and others. I heave a sigh, smack my lips a little, and quickly fall asleep.

CHAPTER 19

We're up before dawn two days later and at Stu's house by 7:00. When Stu meets us at the front door he is cradling a small box under one arm. He greets me with his usual pat on the head and I sniff the box. I didn't know what to expect when they talked about taking Sarah's ashes to Mendocino, but surely this can't be ashes. It doesn't smell human and the box is way too small.

"Better keep the box away from Sam," says Hank. "He's too nosy for his own good."

I'm insulted.

"Why don't you wait by the driveway and I'll back the car out?" Stu says.

I'm excited at the prospect of riding in a big Volvo. Well, maybe it's not so big, but it's luxurious compared to the old VW and the truck. When Stu stops in front of us, Hank opens the back door and arranges the blanket that he has brought to protect the upholstery from my fur.

"You don't need that," says Stu, stepping out of the car. "It's leather; he can't hurt it."

Leather? I'm really traveling first class today.

"You're sure you don't mind driving?" he asks. "It's embarrassing to admit, but I'm just too edgy to drive any long distance these days."

"Hey, no problem." Hank is grinning. "This is a nice change from the VW. And I'm sure Sammy thinks he's died and gone to heaven." Probably not a nice choice of words, considering today's mission, but Hank seems oblivious to his faux pas.

Stu puts the box in the trunk, the men settle themselves into the front seats, and Hank cautiously backs up the car, I glance over at Crabby's house and spot a movement at the front window. Does the woman ever sleep?

Since this is my second trip to Mendocino within a short period of time, I look forward to recognizing familiar scenery. It adds to my feeling of security. I'm rewarded by the sight of cattle alongside the Interstate and I can't help a feeling of superiority as we whiz by. Stupid cows. All they can do is munch grass on the same old hills, while I get to ride past them in an air-conditioned automobile. On a leather seat, yet.

Traffic is light on this early Saturday morning and we zip along with no problem. Zip is the operative word here, and perhaps Hank should have opted for less zip and more concentration on the speedometer, because soon we are followed by a vehicle with flashing red lights.

"Shoot," mutters Hank, slowing and pulling off onto the shoulder. "Oh, hell, Stu, I'm sorry." He turns off the engine, lowers the window and reaches into his pocket for his wallet.

The CHP officer walks slowly to our car, one hand resting on his gun and the other holding a clipboard. He leans down and peers at the three of us.

"Good morning, sir. I'd like to see your driver's license and registration, please."

The words are oh-so-polite and at odds with the imposing uniform standing beside us. The officer is a big guy with an athlete's jaw and dark sunglasses that hide his eyes. His sharply creased shirt fits snugly over the bullet-proof vest.

Hank pulls out his DMV card while Stu retrieves the registration from the glove compartment.

"What seems to be the problem, officer?" says Hank, handing him the papers.

"Sir, you were going pretty fast. I clocked you doing eighty a mile back there."

"I didn't realize that I was going that fast. I'm driving my neighbor here to Mendocino and I guess I'm just not used to judging speed in this car."

"Well, sir, that's why they put speedometers on these things."

The officer bends lower and looks around Hank at Stu. "This your car, sir?"

Stu doesn't look at the man and answers, "Yes."

"I'll be right back with you," says the officer to Hank, attaching the license and registration to his clipboard, and he walks back to his car where he stands behind the open door. Hank and Stu sit in silence while I watch the officer from the rear window. It looks as if he's talking to his shoulder. Soon he returns to us.

Handing the card and registration to Hank, he says, "Sir, I'm writing you a ticket for doing 80 in a 65-mile-per-hour zone. Would you please sign right here."

Hank signs a paper on the clipboard. Handing him a copy, the officer backs away from the car.

"Good morning, sir," he says, "and please drive safely."

I doubt anybody in the U.S. Army says "sir" as much as this guy. In our car it felt as if the entire space had been pressurized, and with the withdrawal of the CHP officer a valve has been opened, deflating us.

The muscles in Hank's jaw are twitching as he carefully merges back onto the freeway. I look at Stu and am astonished to see beads of perspiration glistening on his forehead. Hank notices it, too.

"Hey, Stu, I'm the one who should be sweating here, not you."

Stu pulls out a handkerchief and mops his face. "It's nothing to do with getting a ticket. It's this pressure from the cops—Holcomb and his buddy, especially. Things are so bad I find I'm reacting to the sight of any police officer, even traffic cops. I think I'm losing my grip."

"What are they saying to you? Are they accusing you of anything?"

"No, no, it's not what they say. It's the way they look at me. Like the CHP guy back there. All very polite and everything, but their faces tell another story. Stony. Never crack a smile. And they're always there, watching; know what I mean?"

"You need to get away, go somewhere and relax. Carmel, maybe. Or Tahoe. I have friends with a cabin up there; I could arrange for you to spend some time at their place."

Stu smiles for the first time. "Thanks, but not now. Maybe when the semester ends."

"How are you able to keep your mind on teaching?"

"Like I've said, it takes my mind off this other stuff."

"Think about my offer, anyway." Hank nods his head in satisfaction. "It's something good to look forward to."

Because we left home so early, there's no question about stopping for lunch, but Hank does give us a break halfway through. He pulls off the road at an outdoor market and parks in the shade. We all get out to stretch our legs and Hank gives me water in my portable bowl. I pee on a bush, too, just to let the world know I was here.

The Schuler house is a welcome sight when we finally arrive, road-weary and hungry. Stu retrieves his box from the trunk while Hank gives me another drink of water.

"I dread seeing Emma," says Stu. "Sarah usually made her visits alone. It's been three years since I was here and I know her mother is a lot worse."

To our surprise, the door is opened by a young Filipino woman.

"Good morning," she says. "I'm Maria. Mr. Jack is in the kitchen fixing lunch. Come in. But I think you should leave the dog outside."

What?

"It's okay, Maria," says Hank. "Jack lets Sammy be in the house."

We enter the living room and there she is—ghostly Emma—sitting by the window with her head turned and bowed so low she looks like a sleeping goose.

"I take care of her part-time," says Maria, moving to Emma's side and nudging her shoulder. "Miss Emma? You have visitors."

The head rises, then droops abruptly.

Stu, who has been staring open-mouthed at his mother-in-law, turns at the entrance of Jack from the kitchen.

"You guys have timed this perfectly," says Jack. "Maria is a big help to me and I've been able to put together a lunch for us." He starts to ask a question, but fails to finish it, his eyes on the box clutched in Stu's hands.

Stu stands perfectly still, eyes downcast, and offers the box to Jack. As Jack reaches for it, tears fill his eyes and spill down his cheeks.

"Thank you," he croaks, and carries the box from the room.

There is an awkward silence, broken by unintelligible sounds from Emma.

"She needs to eat," says Maria, scuttling into the kitchen and rattling dishes.

Jack returns quickly, wiping his eyes. "Sorry. It's eerie, knowing I'm holding what's left of my little girl in my hands."

He and Stu embrace for a long moment, until Jack shakes himself, as if ridding himself of emotion. "Come," he says, "lunch is on the table. I don't mean to hurry you, but we have to get to Fort Bragg and the pier. My friend is waiting to take us out. It's just a fishing boat, nothing fancy."

They eat hastily, conversing little, until half way through the meal.

"I forgot to tell you," says Jack. "Pat, my niece in Oregon, called me. She claims that Sarah once told her she thought it would be nice if her ashes could be thrown into the Multnomah Falls. Pat wants to do this as soon as possible."

"We talked it over and I told her we could save some of the ashes for Oregon. But I'm not mailing them and there's no way I can travel there myself. Would you be able to do it, Stu?"

Stu shakes his head. "No way. Not for months."

"I could deliver them for you," Hank says.

"You?" Jack's eyebrows arch themselves in surprise. "But that's a long trip."

"Actually, I need to send a large piece of pottery to a gallery in Portland. The owner is an old friend who has been begging me to show this particular bowl in his store. I've been putting him off because it was going to be such a pain to ship it. Requires careful packing, you know. If I hand deliver it I can take the ashes at the same time."

"It's too much to ask," says Jack.

"I want to do it. Really."

The prospect of a trip to Portland with Hank sets my heart racing. He would never leave me at home. I think.

"I thank you from the bottom of my heart," says Jack, and Stu nods his head in agreement.

The men push themselves from the table, quickly readying themselves for the boat trip. Jack gives last minute instructions to Maria and brings the box from the other room.

"Frankly," he says, "I just want to get this over with."

I position myself at Hank's side, ready for the door to open, but Hank shakes his head at me. "No," he says. "You stay. No dogs allowed on the boat."

My day is ruined. I was so looking forward to riding the waves. And two hours at Jack's with Maria and the ghost lady are not my idea of a good time. I am out of sorts, so I whine at the back door to go out. Maria is reluctant to open the door, but I whine louder and she can't stand it.

The back yard is mostly open field with a few tall trees. I sit down and look around, acutely aware that I am being watched. I look up and there it is: a magnificent red-shouldered hawk sitting on top of the nearest telephone pole. Her powerful beauty stops my heart. We stare at each other and I almost feel as if she is speaking to me. Can dead people's spirits be alive in birds? Is Sarah looking at me? Suddenly, with a great flap of her wings, she takes off. I am alone for a long time.

The returning men walk as if their shoes are made of lead, moving slowly and dragging their feet. I greet them with gusto, but no one pays much attention to me.

"I'm sorry you won't stay for dinner," says Jack. "At least have a cup of coffee for the road."

While Hank and Stu drink in silence, Jack makes two fat tuna fish sandwiches, puts them in lunch bags, and adds bananas and leftover cake. "You'll need this, fellas. On the boat you said you weren't going to stop on the way home, but you have to eat, you know."

He nods toward me. "What about His Royal Highness here? Anything for him?"

"I have dog food in the car," says Hank.

I'd rather have a tuna sandwich and some cake.

As we ready ourselves to leave, Hank and Stu thank Jack profusely and Jack expresses gratitude for their making the trip, but the atmosphere remains dreary and awkward. At the last moment, Jack hands what I now think of as The Box to Hank. "For Portland," he whispers.

In the car Stu inserts a CD into the slot. The entire trip home is filled with music and not much conversation, broken only by our single stop to eat. I sleep most of the way, relishing the pleasure of Stu's leather seats.

CHAPTER 20

Early on our departure day, Stu delivers The Box to our house. I'll be glad when I never have to see it again. Hank packs it behind the back seat with his duffel bag and the boxed pottery he's bringing to the Portland art gallery. Usually I am excited beyond belief at the start of a major trip, but not today. I don't feel that great. Maybe it was something I ate. Like the cat poop I discovered last night covered with dirt near the mailbox.

"What's the matter with you?" says Hank. "You didn't eat your food and now you're moping. This is not the time to get sick on me, Sam."

My response is to jump onto the back seat and lie down with my head on my paws. For most of the day I sleep, oblivious to the scenery, getting out of the car only for water and pee stops.

Early in the evening we register at a dog-friendly motel that Hank has found on the Internet. Apparently he liked it better on the computer screen than in person, because he complains about various amenities, or lack thereof, until we go to bed. As for me, it rates four stars. There are several intriguing stains on the carpet, plus a tantalizing odor in the corner near the bathroom. Female. Exotic. Maybe an Irish setter or even a saluki.

We're up before dawn and I'm feeling quite refreshed after a good night's sleep. I spend the rest of our drive enjoying the scenery, more heavily wooded than our home in California and far less crowded. After a couple hours of this, I fall asleep, awakened eventually by the sound of traffic. We are in Portland.

Hank mutters to himself as he searches for street names and weaves through the traffic. I think he is particularly frustrated by the system of one-way streets, because his swear words increase in frequency and inventiveness. Finally, he eases into a parking spot and grabs his cell phone.

"Pat? It's Hank. I'm parked on 10th Avenue and I can see what I think is your building. Now what?"

Hank listens to a long list of instructions that apparently include being admitted into the parking garage by a man who is loaning us his extra space. Once we are parked in the garage, the man also sees that we get upstairs to the lobby, where the concierge hands Hank a small plastic item that he calls a "fob." He explains how it is used to open doors and to operate the elevator by waving it in front of an electronic eye on the various panels. Hank needs one of these things at home; he could keep his doors continually locked and just open them with a fob. That would make Pete happy.

I am so distracted by my surroundings of glass, chrome, and tasteful art that I almost bump into a tenant dashing through the lobby. To my embarrassment, Hank reprimands me in front of the concierge, a congenial young man who seems to like dogs.

Using the fob is easy, and we are soon on the sixth floor where Pat lives. It is a long wait after ringing the bell before Pat opens the door. No wonder it took her so long; the woman is so obese that she can't move quickly.

Piles of ash blonde hair surround her chubby face, and bright blue eyes check us out. I'll bet she was once a pretty woman, but that was many years and a multitude of pounds earlier.

She beams at Hank, revealing small white teeth. "Oh, Hank, I'm so glad to meet you at last. Sarah told me so much about you," She looks as if she would hug him, thereby suffocating him, probably, but Hank is saved by the presence of The Box in his hand.

"And this is your dog that Sarah talked about. What's his name?"

"Sammy."

She sort of waves a hand in my direction. I think she would like to pat me, but I'm not sure she bends in the middle.

"Welcome to my condominium. This room on your left is the laundry room and there is plenty of space for your bag and clothing."

Sam sets down his duffel bag, along with my supplies, and puts The Box on the counter. Slowly leading us down the long hallway, Pat points out the bathroom and her bedroom. "And here is the living/ kitchen area. You'll sleep on that sofa bed over there."

The large room at the end of her condominium features floor-to-ceiling windows that face 10th Avenue. For once in my life, I can look out a window without standing on my hind legs. I peer down several stories at the people waiting for the streetcar outside the rear of the Portland Art Museum. Tall buildings rise in the distance.

"Have you eaten?" asks Pat. "How about a sandwich? What would you like to drink?" She rattles off each question without giving Hank a chance to answer. "I'll fix us ham sandwiches." She opens the refrigerator. "Now where did I put that meat? There's some beer, I think; no, it's lemonade."

While Pat fumbles about the kitchen, apparently confused about what she keeps and where she keeps it, I wander around the rooms. It could be a stunning condominium if it received some care, but housework is not in Pat's vocabulary. Newspapers, magazines, and books litter the place. Underneath it all is a hardwood floor and some oriental rugs, but only portions of them peek out from the disorder. The only clean and uncluttered spot is a small table in the living room containing a colorful chess set.

"There you are," says Pat, presenting Hank with a lunch of turkey sandwiches and Coke. "And what would Stanley like?"

Stanley?

"His name is Sammy," says Hank, his mouth full, "He'll eat at dinnertime."

"I'm terrible with names," Pat says. "You'll have to excuse me."

She asks for all the details about Sarah's murder and Hank recounts the long story, leaving nothing out. I'm beginning to wonder if Pat is headed down the same road as Sarah's mother, because she makes Hank repeat several bits of information, as if she never heard them the first time.

"You know what?" Pat says. "I think Sarah knew her killer."

"Oh?" Hank stops mid-way raising his Coke to his mouth.

"We talked pretty often on the phone, and the last time I spoke with her she mentioned a person she was concerned about."

Hank's entire body is rigid with attention. "Who?"

"Oh, dear, I'm not sure. It was Art, I think. Art Somebody. A short name. Art Furst? Or maybe it was Forest? And I think he is a potter."

"I know the names of most all the potters in our area and the only one named Art is Art Foyle."

"Maybe that was it."

"I haven't seen any of his work in quite a while. I don't know much about him except that he lives in Willow Glen." Hank's eyebrows rise. "Sarah's office is in Willow Glen. Omigod, this might mean something. Pat, what exactly did Sarah say about him?"

Pat looks as if she wants to cry. "I'm sorry. I wasn't paying close attention to what she said. Mostly I remember that she used the word 'concerned'."

"Okay. Don't worry about it. I'll pass on the information. Now, what about Sarah's ashes? Her dad said you want to scatter them at some falls."

"I was hoping you would go with me late today. If we get there when the crowds are gone, we can do it unobtrusively."

"Sure." Hank's voice lacks enthusiasm. "Just where is this place?"

"Multnomah Falls. A stunning place along the Columbia River Highway. When you see it you'll be glad you're doing this, Hank. And you will understand why Sarah thought it would be a good spot for scattering one's ashes."

"Is it legal?"

"I have no idea and I don't care." Pat tosses her blonde locks in indignation. "Now let me show you the place. I have some pictures in an album somewhere." She heaves herself up from the table and searches through bookshelves. "The Gorge is a lovely, lovely drive and you will enjoy yourself in spite of the occasion. There are at least half a dozen falls along the highway besides Multnomah."

She finds the album after a long search and locates the photo for Hank. "See how that bridge spans the falls? You can walk out on that, but I don't think I'm up to it."

Mission planned, Hank says, "I saw a park near here. I think I should take my dog for a walk."

"Of course. Portland is a dog-friendly city. You can walk right across 10th Avenue and through the walkway at the Art Museum. Be sure to take the fob. Steven will love the park."

Steven?

"Sammy." Hank sighs.

I have a feeling both of us are glad to get out of there. The park proves to be a walker's delight—full of trees, benches to sit on, a gradual hill, college buildings at the upper end, people and dogs all enjoying the outdoors. I gaze up at the overcast sky, wondering if it will rain on us. After so many hours of sitting in a car and then enduring Pat's flightiness, Hank and I set a fast pace around the park's perimeter. It is with reluctance that we return to the condominium.

Pat tells us that it is too early to leave for Multnomah Falls and she suggests a game of chess. Hank, who considers himself quite a whiz at the game, is obviously delighted with the idea. No doubt he views Pat as an easy opponent.

I lie at their feet, listening to the little taps of chess pieces being moved. The two of them play silently, concentrating on the game, and I doze off, awakening when I hear Pat speak.

"Checkmate," she says.

"How'd you do that?" The disbelief in Hank's voice is palpable.

Pat chuckles. "I'll give you a chance to redeem yourself later, if you want. But now it's time to head for the Gorge."

While they ready themselves for the trip, I position myself at the front door. Pat moves slowly, and it is quite a while before we get down to the garage and into her Cadillac. It's a large older model, providing me with even more room than I had in Stu's car. This will make it tough for me to return to Hank's cramped VW.

Pat drives at a snail's pace, oblivious to honking from other cars. I'm sure Hank's teeth must be grinding together, but he doesn't comment. We're caught in the rush hour, too, which doesn't help. After an eternity we escape Portland and the busy Interstate, turning off on our connection to Route 30 and the scenic Columbia River Historic Highway.

"This is beautiful," Hank says, obviously more relaxed.

"Let's stop at Crown Point," says Pat. "It has an unbelievable view."

She takes us up a road leading to a large, round marble building and lookout areas, explaining to Hank the history of the place. As she promised, the vista is spectacular. We see for miles up and down the Columbia River.

"What a gorgeous place," says Hank. "It's easy to understand why the earlier travelers made this their stopping point. And just look at that river. It makes me want to get on a boat and travel its length, just like Lewis and Clark."

I am distracted by the sight of a man who is holding a toy poodle under his arm. When the fellow turns around I am astonished to see that he is a woman. For a female, her shoulders are broad and her hair is cut ultra short. My mistake is understandable; nevertheless, it rattles me that I couldn't tell the gender. As if to scold me, the poodle yaps and squirms in the owner's arms. Dumb dog.

Soon we are back on the highway, where we pass other falls before arriving at Multnomah. There are only two other automobiles in the parking area and the facilities are closed.

"Shall I leave Sammy in the car?" asks Hank.

"It will be all right as long as he is on a leash, and he can stay with me. I can't walk up to that bridge," says Pat.

Hank shoots her a look of disgust. I know he didn't expect to be the dispenser of the ashes.

Pat hoists herself out of the car. Hank carries The Box in one hand and holds my leash in the other as we slowly make our way up toward the falls. It's a magnificent sight, the water cascading from the cliff high above, splashing against the rock wall, filling a pool hidden from our sight, and pouring out again in falls closer to us. We slowly climb the concrete steps to the viewing area. Above and beyond us a narrow bridge spans the pool.

"There," says Pat, pointing at the bridge. "That's where you should scatter the ashes. We're the only ones here, so nobody is going to know what we're doing. Take that path you see on the right; it will lead you up to the bridge."

Hank looks dubious. He hands my leash to Pat and carefully edges open The Box, taking his time, as if he's expecting something to jump out at him.

"Good," he says, with a smile. "Just a few small ashes left in here."

He turns off on the path and Pat finds a spot to sit down. I settle on the pavement beside her, looking for Hank to appear on the bridge. I wish I could be with him up there, but Hank obviously wanted to take care of this by himself. He is on the bridge sooner than I expected. He looks first toward us, then turns around, and we can see him leaning over the rail. Seconds later he walks away. When he reappears from the path Pat lets go of my leash and I dash toward him, leash dragging.

"Hey, Sam, I wasn't gone that long." He scratches my head and his mood is cheerful. I think a weight has been lifted now that his duty is done.

"Sandy certainly adores you," says Pat. "No, that's not right. What is his name again?"

"Sammy."

"My apologies, Sammy." Pat smiles and touches Hank's arm. "Thank you so much, Hank. Sarah would be very pleased with what we've done. Were you able to scatter the ashes okay?"

"Frankly, Pat, it's not the best place to do something like that. It's windy and misty and I'm not sure the ashes even landed in water."

Pat flings an arm around Hank's shoulders and gives him a squeeze. "Never you mind. You did the best you could and that's all that counts."

Later, following a take-out dinner from a market near Pat's place, Hank suggests another game of chess. I know he wants revenge and I suspect that he thinks Pat's prior easy win was a fluke.

Again, I listen to the sound of chess pieces being moved across the board. The game doesn't last long.

"Checkmate," says Pat.

"You're phenomenal," says Hank. "I could never beat you."

Pat is magnanimous in her victory. "Oh, sure, you could. You just need more practice."

Hank swallows hard. He and Stu have played tons of times and Hank wins more often than not.

"Guess we'd better hit the hay," he says. "It's a long trip tomorrow and I need to drop off something at my friend's gallery on the way. We'll be up really early in the morning, so don't bother with us for breakfast."

I'm unsure whether he's refusing breakfast out of kindness to her or whether he's dubious about what she might concoct.

In the morning Hank thanks Pat for her hospitality and she is profuse in her gratitude to him for bringing Sarah's ashes. She's a nice lady, I guess, and a sharp chess player—just a mite confused.

"Goodbye, Stanley," she says, and pats me on the head.

CHAPTER 21

The rest of the day and the next it is rush, rush, rush. Rush to the gallery where Hank's friend meets him and takes delivery of the pottery. Rush to get out of Portland. Rush to get to Medford where we stay at the same motel. Rush home to San Jose. I'm angry at Hank's impatience until it dawns on me: he wants to find Art Foyle, the potter that Pat mentioned.

Hank loses no time once we return home. I hear him on the phone talking to Detective Holcomb, but from the expression on his face I don't think Holcomb is very receptive to his news. Hank provides him with Pat's name and phone number, just in case the lieutenant wants to talk with her.

He makes several calls to other potters, but nobody has any current information on Art Foyle. It's like the man fell off the face of the earth. In the studio Hank hauls out a cardboard box of papers and binders. It is when I hear a loud "Aha!" that I know we are getting somewhere. His next step is to call Ann and invite her to go to lunch in Willow Glen tomorrow. Ann is a pretty shrewd lady and she's getting wise to Hank, I think, because I hear Hank admitting that lunch will be part of what he calls an "investigative trip." Ann doesn't go for Hank's playing detective, but she must have accepted the invitation, anyway, because Hank is whistling when he hangs up.

When Her Nibs arrives the next morning, Hank grabs her in a bear hug and gives her one long juicy kiss. I look away.

"I've missed you, Annie," says Hank. "I wish you could have gone to Portland with me."

"Me, too."

While they are cuddling they seem to be oblivious to the fact that the front door is open, and I seize the opportunity to check out the neighborhood. When Hank took me for my walk earlier, nobody was about, but now I spot Bud Manolo across the street watering his lawn. I haven't seen Bud since last weekend when we discovered he writes poetry. I've missed his pungent smells, so I dash across the street. Since Crabby lives next door to him, I expect to hear her yell at me, but there is no sound. She must be on the phone, or something. Truth to tell, it is more fun when she sees me and is upset with my behavior.

"Hey, there, Sammy," says Bud, shutting off his hose. "Come give me a kiss."

I oblige him with a slurp right on the puss. This beats any kiss between Hank and Ann; Bud's face tastes of egg and bacon grease. I lick his lips, chin, cheeks, and nose. Might as well get some salt to go with the egg.

"Hey, Buddy." Bud laughs and pushes me away. "Enough, already." A little saliva escapes with his words. I think he's missing some dentures today.

"Sammy! Come!"

I don't like the tone of Hank's voice and I skedaddle back across the street immediately.

"What's got into you?" Hank grabs me under the jaw and looks me in the eye. "You know better than that."

Oh, well, getting a taste of Bud Manolo was worth it.

"I've a good mind to leave you home today."

Then again, maybe it wasn't worth it.

It is Ann who saves me later when she urges Hank to allow me to accompany them. Hank gives in and I vault happily into the back seat of the Volkswagen. In no time at all, we reach Willow Glen, an older area of San Jose with large shady trees and unique homes, many with stucco exteriors and Spanish tile roofs. Some of them are what Hank says are Craftsman style.

Ann helps Hank find an address on Pine St. "What a darling house," she says, when we stop in front of a tile-roofed home with a carefully tended yard. "If this Foyle person you're looking for is anything like his house, he must be a nice guy. What are you going to say to him, anyway, Hank? 'I looked you up because I think you killed somebody'?"

"Aw, c'mon, Annie."

"Really. This is not your role, you know. And I don't think the detective would like it very much if he knew you were here."

"It'll be okay, don't worry."

When Ann gets out of the car I jump out, too, and follow them to the front door. Hank doesn't seem to notice.

The doorbell is answered by a Mexican-American lady wearing a flowered apron and bright yellow plastic gloves. She narrows her eyes at Hank, but then relaxes when she sees Ann.

"Good morning," says Hank. "I'm looking for Art Foyle. Does he still live here?"

"No. He went to live with his daughter a few months ago. We are renting."

"I see." The disappointment shows on Hank's face. "Do you happen to have his daughter's address? It's very important that I reach him."

The lady looks down at me, but doesn't answer.

"I'm a potter like he is, or at least he was the last I knew," says Hank.

Perhaps she is reassured that a man with a friendly dog and a pretty woman is to be trusted. She says, "Momentito," and closes the door.

"I think we're supposed to wait," says Hank. "Let's hope."

"I think we're supposed to forget the whole idea," says Ann.

"And you," says Hank, giving me a poke, "why aren't you in the car?"

We don't wait long before the door reopens and the lady hands Hank a piece of paper. "This is the address. Good-by." She closes the door abruptly.

"And good-by to you," says Hank.

"You can't blame the woman," says Ann. "After all, we're a couple of strangers knocking on her door."

Back in the car, Hank unfolds his map and locates the address. "Hey, it's still in Willow Glen and not far from here. We just have to go up Pine to Hicks and Hicks becomes Camino Ramon."

Once we are on Camino Ramon, Hank asks Ann to help him check the numbers. Our destination turns out to be on the other side of Minnesota Avenue.

"What lovely homes," says Ann. "I wouldn't mind living here."

We pull up in front of a large stucco house with a walled patio in the front, shaded by huge sycamores. The wall is low enough that we can make out two figures sitting there. As we approach on the sidewalk, one gets up to greet us. She's a young woman with long black hair and a friendly-looking face.

"Can I help you?" she asks.

"Morning," says Hank. I'm Hank Arrowby and this is my friend, Ann Schaefer. I'm looking for Art Foyle. Are you his daughter?"

The face clouds. "Yes, I am. Does he know you?"

"I'm not sure. I'm a potter like he is and he may know of me, but I can't recall if we've met."

"What is it you want?" The face lightens up, but the words are measured.

The sudden appearance of a little boy, running out from behind the patio wall, saves Hank from responding.

"Mommy! Mommy!" The little tyke stops short when he spies me and his face lights up. "Doggie!" He stumbles toward me, hands outreached.

Fortunately for me, the woman stoops to prevent his onward rush. "No, no, Stevie," she says. "Wait until you're told it's okay to pet the dog."

"Sam is good with children," says Hank.

Shoot. I submit to clumsy pats on the head while Hank peers beyond the daughter at the man still seated behind the wall. "Is that your dad there?"

"Yes. And why is it, Mr. Arrowby, that you want to see him?" This lady is like a tail-wagging guard dog—friendly acting, but barring the way, nevertheless.

"Actually, I wanted to ask him some questions about a woman we both know."

"I'm afraid that's impossible."

"Impossible?"

"My father had a stroke six months ago. He's unable to speak or write." She turns toward the patio, beckoning us to follow. "Come and meet him, anyway. It will be good stimulation for him. And by the way, my name is Alice."

Hank is frozen in place. Surprise registers on his face and Ann has to nudge him forward.

"Daddy? Look, Daddy, some people are here to see you." Alice's voice is artificially perky. "Do you remember Hank Arrowby?"

Mr. Foyle pays no attention to Hank and Ann, but his eyes zero in on me. The left side of his mouth droops and his left arm lies curled and lifeless in his lap. "Unhh," he says, staring at me.

"Maybe you could bring your dog close to him," Alice says to Hank.

"Sure," says Hank, who apparently has recovered from his initial shock. "Sammy, heel." We walk smartly up to the man and Hank has me sit.

"Unhh," says Mr. Foyle, briefly gesturing toward me with his right hand. The hand plops back in his lap and he looks away.

Alice's eyes glisten. "That is the most interest he's shown since he came to live with us. More even than with Stevie. Won't you sit down?" She gestures toward the vacant chairs.

Hank glances at Ann before answering. "I'm sorry. I only intended to be here briefly to ask your father a couple questions. We can't stay."

"I understand," says Alice. "Thank you, anyway, for taking your dog up to him. Maybe we should get a dog."

Hank gives her a weak smile, they say their good-bys, and we retreat to the Volkswagen.

Ann pats Hank on the shoulder. "Guess that takes care of that suspect."

"Nuts," is Hank's response, and he drives us in silence to a delicatessen on Lincoln Avenue.

"They have great meatball sandwiches here," he says, ushering us to a tiny table near the parking lot. He ties my leash to a table leg. "Guard our table, Sammy," He and Ann enter the deli, leaving me wondering what I'm supposed to do if some strangers try to sit down here. Bite them?

Nobody bothers me, and Hank and Ann soon return, carrying plates that set me drooling instantly. Meat. Heavenly, rapturous, ravishing meat.

"It pays to be early," says Hank. "At noon time the line will be out the door."

They settle themselves in the chairs and I move closer to Hank. "Hey," he says, "you're drooling on my pants. Sit." I sit immediately and am rewarded with a meatball dripping with sauce. "That's it; that's all you get."

I turn away and edge toward Ann. I focus on the sandwich in her hand, and when she eyes me I look away, trying to appear uninterested. She bursts out laughing.

"You big faker!" she says. "Okay. Sit." She tosses me a gloppy meatball. "I can't resist those big brown eyes." Maybe Her Nibs has some redeeming qualities, after all.

"I keep going over what Pat said," says Hank. "How did she get it so wrong?"

"She actually said his name? Art Foyle?"

"I know she said 'Art' and she wasn't sure about the last name. She thought it started with 'F', it was a short name, and Sarah told her she was concerned about the guy. Pat also believed he was a potter."

"So how did she come up with 'Foyle'?"

"Come to think of it, I was the one who said 'Foyle'. I knew of a potter named Art Foyle who lived in Willow Glen, the same area where Sarah had an office. It seemed to be too much of a coincidence. Then again, I should have known that Pat wouldn't have the name right. She's real flighty. Great chess player, though."

"Maybe Sarah was talking about Arthur, not Art. Arthur Foyt. Isn't that Brick's real name?"

"Sheesh! You're right. Plus Sarah, being a therapist, would naturally have concerns about him. She went out of her way to be nice to him."

"And Sarah would have mentioned a potter, meaning you."

Hank shakes his head back and forth. "Damn! What an ass I've been."

"Not an ass, honey," says Ann, and she reaches forward to lay a hand on his. "Just an over-eager would-be private eye."

"Same thing," says Hank, and he manages a sheepish grin.

"I've missed you."

Oh, please. The woman saw him a week ago; what more does she want?

"Let's go on a hike, since the weather has cooled off so much. I feel like some exercise after all the driving I've done this week. How about Tuesday?"

"I thought you couldn't hike."

"It's a park that's more of a stroll than a real hike."

My spirits lift when Her Nibs agrees, not that I want her around, but it will be good to sniff new territory.

CHAPTER 22

While Hank is watering on the morning of our hike, he discovers the watering wand is broken, which means a quick trip to the hardware store, a short distance from our house. Hardware stores—paradise for men, and dogs, too, for that matter. Nothing prissy or cutesy about a hardware store. Plain, utilitarian, and a treasury of manly smells, each section of the store with its own special aroma.

Take the gardening department, for example, where Hank heads first. My favorite. All that organic compost just waiting to be sniffed. I plant my nose squarely on a box of All-Purpose and inhale deeply.

"Get away from there." Hank tugs at the leash. The man has no appreciation for fertilizer odors.

He can't prevent my sniffing the air, however; so, while he examines a watering wand, I sit in the middle of the aisle and raise my nose toward the ceiling. The odors swirl through the air. Bone meal. Ammonia. Paint. Tobacco breath. Linseed oil. A familiar human odor.

Where have I smelled this? The memory kicks in simultaneously with the appearance of Blondie, that mean guy from Skyline, at the end of the aisle. All the hairs on my neck stand on end. Blondie has spotted us and his eyes narrow, but Hank is engrossed in the watering gadget. I growl.

Hank whirls around. At the sight of Blondie he pales ever so slightly. Blondie abruptly turns away, but I have the feeling he's faking a lack of interest.

Hank plunks the watering wand plus a soaker hose into the cart and heads in the opposite direction from Blondie. We meander down three aisles, Hank browsing among plumbing fixtures, until we find the aisle with felt pads. As Hank reaches for a box, movement at the aisle's end catches my eye. I growl a second time. Hank looks up, but misses the sight of Blondie, who ducks away the instant I look at him.

"Cool it, Sam," Hank says.

Cool, schmool. I want out of here.

In the parking lot there is no sign of Blondie, but my relief is short-lived. After exiting onto Carlton I look out the rear window and there he is, right behind us, driving a dinged-up, old Ford truck. Quickly I turn away and start whining.

"What's your problem?" Hank checks me in his rear view mirror, then looks ahead. Back and forth as we drive down Carlton, he alternates between the street and the mirror, until finally I realize that he has spotted Blondie behind us. I keep hoping that ugly man will turn off, but Blondie sticks with us. I worry what will happen when we get home.

But Hank has no intention of showing Blondie where he lives. He drives right past Cowper all the way to Union and turns right. I keep hoping that a traffic light will separate us, but luck is on Blondie's side. Even when Union ends steeply at Blossom Hill Road, there is no cross traffic and Blondie stays right with us on the turn. Hank mutters under his breath. In spite of trying to time it so that he leaves Blondie behind when a light changes from yellow to red, he can't shake the man. Blondie hangs on like a damn tick.

Only after traveling almost to Los Gatos Boulevard do I realize Hank's intention. He's going to escort Blondie right to the police station. Blondie must have come to the same conclusion, because he suddenly zooms past us, middle finger raised high.

Hank laughs. As for me, I lie down on the back seat and pant rapidly all the way home. I'm not cut out for this.

Because of his gimpy leg, Hank has to stick to easy walking, which limits our choice of parks. One of the best is Oak Grove Guadalupe Park, home to lots of shady oak trees on a flat area. Acorn woodpeckers galore flit about through the trees, squawking at each other. There is a hilly section, some of it steep, and another part more gradual, which Hank is able to navigate with his cane. It's to this last area that we head, rewarded by a great sight of a beautiful bird perched on a snag. It has a rusty colored back with black stripes, a spotted chest, and a face that looks as if it has a moustache.

"Look," says Hank, "there's a kestrel!"

"It looks like a small hawk," Ann says.

"Close. It's a falcon. This is worth the whole hike."

"Lucky us," says Ann.

"I can't get over how uncrowded the park is today," says Hank. "I suppose because it's Tuesday. We've only seen half a dozen people so far."

Half way across the hill, Hank stops and hands the leash to Ann. "I've got something in my shoe. Hold him, would you?"

It's at that precise moment of leash transfer that I spot a ground squirrel going hell-bent-for-leather across the trail and toward some boulders. It's as if my mind and body have separated; my nerves and muscles respond automatically while my brain is devoid of any reasonable thought. I give chase right into the opening where three boulders join together and I come to an immediate and painful stop, smashing my nose on a rock inside. It's pitch black in this minute cave and it smells of dirt and decay. To my dismay, when I attempt to back out I discover that my right front paw is wedged between two rocks, holding me prisoner in the dark. Pain shoots up my foreleg.

Now I hear shouts from Hank and Ann. "Sammy!" And from Hank, "Damn dog!"

Ann reaches me first. "He's way in there, Hank." Her voice sounds a little panicky. "Don't worry, Sam, we'll get you out. Good dog." Her hands are patting my rear end. She must be on her hands and knees.

Hank finally arrives. Breathlessly, he asks, "Is he stuck?"

I try frantically to move my paw and whimper in pain as I attempt to pull it out.

"Poor dog. Take it easy, sweetheart. You'll be okay." Ann strokes my rump again with her fingertips and she sniffles. Is she crying? "Hank, you've got to get him out."

Hank's voice sounds choked, like he's trying to swallow a dog biscuit whole. "I can't. Ann, I can't. It's the claustrophobia." His voice is rising in pitch and now so is Ann's.

"I'll do it. I'm smaller than you are, anyway, so it should be easier."

Without waiting for further word from him, she wriggles herself into the cave, partly on top of me and partly on the side. "Easy, Sammy, easy. Good boy."

I can feel her stretch along my body and her hand slides down my foreleg, stopping just before the point where I'm trapped.

"I can't reach it. My arm's not long enough." Now I know she's crying.

She backs out of the cave. What if they can't rescue me? What if I'm left to die here? My nose is full of dirt and my paw throbs, pains shooting up the leg when I try to move it the slightest bit.

There is quiet behind me, punctuated by a few murmurs, and then I feel Hank's presence at my rear. He's breathing hard and grunting as he squeezes his torso into the tight space. He's heavier than Ann, but I don't care;

anything, as long as he can free my paw. His hand slides down my leg, just as Ann's did, but it reaches my paw and his fingers investigate the entrapment.

"Gotta move it forward and then to the side," he whispers. I struggle when he stretches my leg forward and then tries to slide it. "Easy, Sam," he says. The leg doesn't move. A second attempt and still no result. He's grunting with the effort, his sweat dripping on my head. "Ah!" The paw is freed.

I don't know which one of us wants out of that place the most. We both squirm and wriggle and then we're in daylight. As Hank starts to stand up, Ann envelops us both in her arms.

"You did it! You did it." Tears are streaming down her face. "Oh, no. He's bleeding. His paw is a mess. And look at that nose. Oh, my poor baby." And then she's kissing me. Big smacky kisses.

I melt.

For the first time I get a look at Hank's face. Streaks of dirt darken his nose and cheeks, and a scratch across his forehead is bleeding. His eyes are clouded with concern.

I try to take a step, but the sharp pain makes me squeal.

Ann squats to check my paw more closely. Her face isn't much better than Hank's; the only difference is that her eyes are red from crying. I give her a lick right on the lips.

"C'mon, Sam," Hank says, grunting, as he hefts me up to his shoulder. We'll make this a semi-fireman's carry."

"Are you sure you can do this?" says Ann.

"Carry my cane, would you?"

Lurching along on Hank's shoulder is not much better than limping myself and I struggle to get down. Hank squats while Ann helps lift me off. Fresh blood splotches Hank's shirt and Ann's as well—dark red decorations that follow no pattern.

I use the pause in our progress as an opportunity to lick my bleeding paw. The blood is salty and quite tasty, a bonus to the pleasure I get from the rhythmic strokes of my tongue. I struggle when Hank once again hoists me to his shoulder, causing him to return me to the ground.

"This is not working," he says. "I'll get the emergency blanket from the car. You stay with him."

Ann sits on the ground, stroking my side until I become more aware of her touch and less aware of the pain. With a grunt I turn to lay my head in her lap. Her strokes extend now from the top of my head, along my flank, all the way to my hip."

"Such a good dog." The words caress me. I close my eyes, dozing, until Hank returns with the blanket.

They use it like a stretcher, but it's far from a smooth trip, what with Hank's limping and Ann's difficulty holding up her end. The bleeding has stopped by the time we reach the car and I manage to put some weight on the injured leg; however, jumping into the back seat of the Volkswagen is impossible, so Hank and Ann heft and heave me into the vehicle. I lie down on the seat, uninterested, for once, in looking out the window.

Once home, they lift me from the car. I surprise us all by walking unaided into the house, although it hurts my paw to step on it.

I knew it. Hank is on the phone to the vet immediately. This will mean a visit to that horror chamber—the veterinary clinic. It's not that the staff isn't pleasant; it's the smell that gets me every time. I try to disappear behind the sofa, but to no avail. Hank spots me and helps me to the car. I exaggerate my limp and he laughs when he picks me up to carry me the rest of the way.

"How come you could walk into the house, but not out? You don't fool me, Sammy."

I relax pretty well lying down on the back seat and when Hank lifts me out of the car I've convinced myself that this office visit will be a piece of cake. What a strange expression: piece of cake. Perhaps if I were given a slice it would make sense.

Hank carries me into the clinic where my entire pretense at calmness vanishes. It's that smell: antiseptic; clinical; death has occurred here. I tremble in spite of Hank's arms around me.

"Perfect timing," says Millie, the clerk. "We've just had a no-show and Dr. Cummins will be able to see you immediately."

I wish *I* were a no-show.

Apparently Millie doesn't want Hank to carry me anymore, because she wheels out a table to transport me to the exam room. Even though Hank's walk is jolting, I'd rather have that with his arms around me than lie on this hard cold thing. In the exam room I'm transferred to another table where I shake more than ever. Dr. Cummins enters right away.

"So, what happened to our boy?" he asks.

He lays one of his large warm hands on my shoulder. Immediately I am calmed and I suppress the whimper that is threatening to escape my throat.

Hank describes our ordeal as Dr. Cummins runs his hands over my entire body, ending with the injured paw. I pull back in pain.

"I don't think anything's broken," he says, "but we'd better x-ray it."

He lifts me and carries me to another room where the x-ray machine is. His veterinary technician, someone I don't know, helps with the procedure. I work hard to co-operate and lie still, because I don't want to be anesthetized. It is soon over and I'm back with Hank, where we wait for the x-ray to be read.

When Dr. Cummins returns to the exam room he is smiling. "No fracture," he says. "All that pressure on the paw from being wedged in the rock has caused swelling, and that in turn is what is causing his pain. He should be a lot better tomorrow. Dogs panic when they get trapped, you know, so they think they're hurt more than they are. If you don't act over-concerned, he'll recover faster."

What? I'm insulted. When Dr. Cummins sets me on the floor, I turn my back and head for the door, trying my darndest not to limp.

"See? He's better already."

I refuse to look anybody in the eye, and when we stop at the desk to pay the bill, I turn up my nose at the treat offered by Millie.

Home again, we find Ann preparing a tasty snack. When Hank catches her sneaking me a piece of cheese he doesn't say a word, even though he ordinarily won't allow anyone to give me people food. For the rest of the day all three of us decompress and by the time Ann leaves, life is almost back to normal.

CHAPTER 23

"How would you like to go to Carmel tomorrow?" Hank is on the phone with Ann. "We could check out some galleries, have lunch—you know, be like normal people. Sammy is much better already, and it would do us all good to get away."

Get away. Ever since the memorial service two weeks ago, it seems as if Hank has been trying to get away. First it was to Mendocino, then Portland, now Carmel. I think he's trying to get away from reality—the reality he faces each time he looks at the house next door.

We pick up Ann at her apartment in Campbell where I wait in the car. On his return Hank laughs at something Ann says and pulls her to him, giving her a smack on the top of her curly head. It's the sort of confident, casual gesture that bespeaks intimacy and happiness. A week ago it would have sickened me, but now I thump my tail at the sight.

"Hi, Sammy, sweetie," says Ann as she settles into the VW. I thump my tail harder.

It's enjoyable, for once, to drive over the mountain with no agenda but fun. Passing by the artichoke fields in Castroville, Hank comments that we must buy some chokes on the way back. My side window is open a crack and I stick my nose into it for a whiff, but the rushing air stings my nostrils, so I settle for views out the window, instead. When we slow down through Moss Landing I wish we were stopping here, rather than going to Carmel with its trendy shops. Moss Landing is alive with fishermen and families and boats and birds and dogs. Without putting my nose to the window I can smell the fish and the salt air. My kind of place.

Hank picks up speed again and soon we are treated to the sight of Monterey Bay with its white surf and breathtaking blue water. The gods have smiled on us. It's usually foggy here in the summer, at least in the mornings, but today is bright and clear—perfect, made-to-order weather on the California coast.

We come to a halt upon reaching Ocean Street, main drag into Carmel. The town is a tourist Mecca, especially on a Saturday, which means we crawl through traffic. We cruise up and down residential streets a very long time looking for a parking space. Ann amuses herself checking out the famous storybook houses while Hank curses every time he thinks he has found a spot, only to discover it is a driveway.

Parked at last, a new search begins. Hank knows a French restaurant with patio seating, but of course he can't remember what street it's on. Up and down the shop-lined streets we trudge. This had better be worth it.

"Aha," says Hank. "Here we go."

He opens a gate leading into a small brick patio in front of the restaurant. We haven't gone five steps before we hear "Hank! Over here."

Stu Fetzler is waving from an umbrella-shaded table. The lady seated beside him looks familiar.

"Stu? What are you doing here?" Surprise registers in Hank's voice.

"You both remember Vera Escobar, I think," says Stu. "You met at Hank's." To Vera he says, "Hank Arrowby and Ann Schaefer."

"Oh, yes, you're the councilwoman," says Ann.

Vera gives her a dazzling smile. "You both did a marvelous job with that reception."

"Vera was a life saver today, "says Stu. "She suggested we come to Carmel to work on the theater proposal instead of sitting in hot San Jose. Just what I needed, because I was down in the dumps."

"You work on Saturday?" Hank says to Vera.

"Whenever," says Vera. "We politicians don't know one day from the next." She flashes sparkling teeth at Hank. "It was my idea to combine an outing to Carmel with work. I thought Stuart could use a change of scenery."

"Good thinking," says Hank.

"Care to join us?" asks Stu.

"Thanks, I don't think so. We've got the dog, you know."

"Well, enjoy your meal. The food here is marvelous." Vera flashes another of her remarkable smiles. That woman's teeth are so glowing she could ride a bicycle in the dark and not need a light.

We find a table in a corner near a pink flowering bush, and a young waitress with short-cropped black hair soon approaches us. She looks as if she came directly from the Left Bank of Paris.

Hank must have the same thought, because he asks her, "Do you have a bowl of water for le chien?"

"For what?" she asks.

"He means the dog," says Ann, and Hank flushes.

"Of course," says the girl, giving me a pat. "As long as the dog is only in the patio."

When she leaves after taking the orders, Ann gives Hank a poke in the arm. "Le chien," she mimics. "You goofball."

"Well, she looked French."

"People aren't always what they seem. Take Vera Escobar, for instance."

"What do you mean?"

"She doesn't care about the theater project. She has her hooks into Stu."

"Aw, c'mon, Annie." Hank shakes his head in protest. "She's done a lot to help bring affordable cultural stuff to that East Side community. Theirs is a working relationship. You only met the woman twice. How can you make that snap judgment?"

"Easy. A woman knows."

"I think you're crazy." Hank stares at Vera and Stu eating their salads. "Anyway, Stu isn't the type to fall for somebody like that. Sarah was his true love. Besides, it's too soon since her death."

"You're naive, Hank."

The muscles in Hank's jaw are flexing—not a good sign——and I'm worried that they'll have a spat and leave before I get my water dish. I'm saved by the appearance of the waitress with a bowl of water and a doggie biscuit, for which I willingly sit and look appropriately grateful.

The two of them have little to say to each other until the waitress returns with their orders. I notice that Hank frequently looks over at Stu and Vera, quietly observing. Eventually he just shakes his head and apologizes to Ann. There's nothing like a little tiff to make the heart grow stronger, apparently, because now Hank and Ann act all lovey-dovey like a pair of newlyweds.

On the way home Hank says, "I'll show you where Windsor Huddleston lives." He exits onto Summit Road.

"Hank?" Ann is frowning. "Aren't you getting a little bit obsessive about this? "

The jaw muscles are flexing again. "I'm not obsessive, I'm just being observant. He needs to know he can't get away with anything."

"Be reasonable. The man isn't even under suspicion, as far as we know."

"He's under my suspicion."

"Oh, for heaven's sake!" Ann is ticked.

Hank slows down as we pass Huddleston's home. At the same moment, Hud appears from around the side of his house and stops mid-stride to watch us driving by.

"He sees us," says Ann.

"Good." Hank smirks.

"This is so embarrassing."

Ann folds her arms, clamps her mouth shut, and doesn't say one word the rest of the way. What is it with human couples?

When Hank exits Highway 17 onto 85, Ann breaks the silence. "Where are you going?"

"Home."

"Your home, you mean. Maybe I don't want to go there, did you consider that?

"Aw, honey, let's not fight. How about we just hang out at the house and then I cook you something special for dinner. What do you say?"

Ann says nothing.

"Please?" Hank shoots her a look and then grins. "A real gourmet surprise from chef Arrowby?"

Ann turns to look at Hank and he must have a pathetic expression on his face, because she bursts out laughing.

"Even when I want to, I can't stay mad at you, Hank Arrowby."

"It's my sophisticated charm," says Hank, and they both laugh.

When we arrive home Mrs. Crawford calls to us from across the street before the car doors are even closed. "Hank!" she hollers, and waves him over.

"I'll make sure this is brief," Hank tells Ann, and I trot along with him off leash to see what Crabby wants.

"Don't let him near that rose bush," she says, meaning me. Heck, I'm not even looking at the damn thing.

"Freda Hoyt was at your house looking for you," Crabby says.

"Oh-oh," mutters Hank, under his breath.

I hope Hank is not in trouble.

"What did she want, Mrs. Crawford?"

"Well, I don't know, do I? I'm not a mind reader." Crabby purses her lips to look more chicken-like than ever. "I saw her ring your doorbell and I simply thought you'd like to know,"

Who needs an alarm system when Crabby Crawford lives in your neighborhood?

"Okay," says Hank.

Back at the house, he assures Ann he'll only be a minute at the Hoyt's. "I may as well get this over with; otherwise, she'll be down here again."

When Freda Hoyt answers the doorbell she steps outside and closes the door behind her. "I don't want Arthur to hear me," she explains. "Hank, I'm upset with you. I'm sure you told the police that Arthur had a piece of Sarah Fetzler's jewelry in his collage, because they brought him down to the Sheriffs Department a second time for more questioning. He was there for hours and he came home extremely agitated. Arthur is not completely right in the head, you know that, but he is no murderer. He had nothing to do with Sarah's killing."

Hank touches Mrs. Hoyt's arm. "I'm sorry, Freda, really. I felt I had no choice but to inform the detectives. You must admit, when a woman is murdered and a brooch of hers shows up in someone's artwork, then that is something that needs to be followed up. It doesn't mean your son killed her, but it does require an explanation."

"Arthur picks up things everywhere. He probably found it near their house."

"Has he told you where he got it?"

"I don't want to ask him, because he is already so upset about the detectives' questioning. If Arthur goes off the deep end and has to be hospitalized, it's your fault, Hank." Mrs. Hoyt gives a sniff and stomps back into her home.

When we return to Ann she instantly spots a change in Hank's demeanor. "What happened? You look as if Mrs. Foyt gave you a going-over. Were you a bad boy?" She grins and pats the seat cushion next to her on the sofa. "Sit down and confess your sins."

"Freda's mad at me because Brick got hauled down for more questioning, and she knows I told the detectives that Brick had Sarah's butterfly pin in one of his collages. I can't believe Brick murdered Sarah. He's a fruitcake, but..." Hank shakes his head. "I still think Hud is involved. And then there are those weird guys on Skyline. I forgot to tell you—one of them was at the hardware store the morning we went hiking. He followed me in the car and I got rid of him by pretending I was headed for the Los Gatos police station."

"Hank! What am I going to do with you?" Ann looks truly distressed. "I'm afraid you're going to put yourself in danger. I don't want to lose you." Her voice catches on the last word.

Hank's response is to hold her tightly and start kissing her all over her face. I quietly slink off to a corner because I know darn well what's coming and I hope Hank can't see me. No such luck. Hank drags me into the studio and shuts the door.

Damn!

By the time Hank returned from taking Ann home last night, it was almost midnight, leading me to hope that today he would want to sleep in, or at least just putter around the house. Instead, he is back on his sleuthing obsession, which means that once again we drive to the Santa Cruz Mountains. I hope that he won't be so foolish as to try tailing Huddleston, but no such luck; we drive to Summit Road, parking in the shade a little ways from the house. Hud's truck is in the driveway. I adjust my hope—maybe Hud will stick to his house and we can just go home.

Shoot. In only half an hour he emerges from the house, putters around in the front yard for a bit, then takes off in the truck with us following a discreet distance behind. This is getting ridiculous.

After about a mile, Hud turns onto a narrow road, which quickly dead ends, and he abruptly stops. We're trapped.

There is no way to pass him. Hank's only choice is to park behind. Hud is out of his truck and at Hank's window in a flash.

"Arrowby, what the hell do you think you're doing? You crazy bastard, you're following me everywhere!" He leans on the window, shoving his face close to Hank's. His eyes narrow to slits and his words hiss through nicotine-stained teeth. "Cut it out or I'm pressing charges."

"Maybe I have a reason for keeping my eye on you." Hank's voice is steady.

"What reason? Because Sarah and I had a thing years ago? You nuts?"

"Because of your actions, Hud."

If Huddleston comes any closer to Hank he might as well get in the car. Hank has to lean back.

"Actions? What actions? The hell you talking about?"

"You were up at the place where Sarah's body was found, for starters."

"So? You were there, too. Maybe you were returning to the scene of the crime." Hud smiles in a sickly way.

Hank lets the comment slide over him. "And then you met some guy in Santa Cruz. I saw you hand him a package."

Hud throws back his head and guffaws, startling Hank and me. When he finally stops laughing he gives Hank a little punch on the shoulder.

"You're an asshole, you know that? That was one of the retired guys from Station 26. He lives in Santa Cruz. I was bringing him some old photos of Fred Rourke for Fred's retirement party."

Hud leans on the door again. And now his face darkens. "Hank, you should get some therapy. You're a sick man." He spins on his heels and walks away, shaking his head.

Hank drops his head onto the steering wheel. "Oh, God," he says, and hits the wheel with his hand.

We drive home in silence.

While he's preparing dinner, Hank turns on the small TV that he keeps in the kitchen. The local news is on and occasionally he looks up from the stove, but mostly he doesn't pay much attention. Until, that is, he hears the name Stuart Fetzler, and then he jerks his head up so fast he hits it on the hood of the vent. The anchor is going on and on about the Fetzler case and how there have been no arrests but they haven't ruled anyone out yet. They run the same pictures of Stu taken outside his home when Sarah was first known to be missing. Stu's handsome face crumples as he answers the reporter's questions about Sarah. There are shots of the neighborhood, too, including our house, taken at the same time. The anchor makes it sound as if Stu is a suspect.

Hank is as upset as I am and he grabs the phone to call Stu. Apparently he gets the answering machine.

"Hey, Stu," he says, "you were on the news again tonight. I'm sorry, guy. Come on over if you want to escape nosy reporters or just have a beer or something."

Knowing how Stu screens his calls these days, we expect him to pop in, if not at the moment, then later, but he doesn't show.

CHAPTER 24

In the morning Hank gets out the mower and the edger to tackle the front yard. I sniff around the bushes, looking for the scent of someone I know, but all I smell is opossum and a couple cats. I look up to see the Meissner's teen-age son, Anthony, approaching, but Hank doesn't notice him until he's onto the lawn. The orange stripe is gone, and today his hair is spiked with the ends colored blond. He's wearing a small hoop earring in his left ear that I think is new.

"Mr. Arrowby?" says Anthony.

"Hey, Anthony." Hank stops and leans on the mower. "How's it going?"

"Okay. Um, Mr. Arrowby, could I, um, talk to you?"

"Sure, Anthony. What is it?"

Anthony bites his lip and sways a little from side to side.

"Ah, well, I, uh...." This kid is making me nervous. I wish he'd just spit it out.

"Listen, why don't we go inside and talk," says Hank, who must feel the same way. "It's cooler in there. How'd you like a Coke?"

"Yeah, thanks."

While Hank gets Cokes out of the refrigerator Anthony walks nervously around the kitchen, looking at pictures and out the window at the back yard.

"Thanks," he says, as they sit down at the table and Hank hands him the can. Anthony takes a gulp and then sits staring into the can opening as if he expects the words to come to him out of the Coke.

"What is it, Anthony?" asks Hank.

"I need to tell you something." Anthony lifts his head and now he stares straight at Hank. "But you gotta promise me you won't tell my father. He'll kill me if he finds out."

Hank shakes his head. "How can I promise you when I don't know what it is?"

The kid looks away and for a moment there is silence.

Abruptly, Hank asks, "Anthony, is this about the mailboxes?"

Anthony swings his head back to look at Hank and his jaw drops open. "How did you know?"

"Wild guess." I can tell that Hank is suppressing a smile.

"Please, oh, please don't tell my dad. I'll mow your lawn, I'll weed your back yard, I'll do anything to pay you back for trashing the mailbox. I'm sorry I did it."

Hank cocks his head and narrows his eyes. "Why are you telling me this now? People fixed their mailboxes long ago and I had no reason to suspect you were behind the vandalism. Are you suddenly feeling guilty?"

"No. I mean, yes. I mean I feel a little guilty, but that's not the reason I'm telling you."

"What's the reason?"

"I need to tell you what I saw that night and now you know why I was in your yard at 1:00 in the morning."

"I don't understand."

"I saw him that night."

"I still don't understand. What night? Who?"

"Mr. Fetzler. The night Mrs. Fetzler disappeared."

Now it's Hank's jaw that is dropping open. "What did you see, Anthony? Start from the beginning."

"Well, it's like this. Me and Jeff Wilkins had been doing the mailboxes together. It was just on a dare at first and then, I dunno, it was exciting or something, and we kept doing it. I know, it was stupid. Anyway, after we'd done your mailbox Jeff went back down Cowper to go home, but I didn't want anybody on our street to see me, so I went to the corner in front of Fetzler's house. Then I was going to go down Branham and around the block to my house. I was keeping to the bushes and when I got to the corner I saw Mr. Fetzler walking down Branham from the other direction. He unlocked his gate and went in to his yard from the Branham side."

Hank sits staring at Anthony.

"Who else knows this?"

"Nobody. I was afraid to say anything because then everybody would know I'd done the mailboxes. And it didn't seem that important. But there was stuff on TV last night about the case, and I got to thinking maybe I should say something. To you, anyway."

Hank is looking a little pale and I'm on high alert, myself.

"Listen, Anthony," says Hank. "Don't say anything to anybody just yet, okay? I'm sure there must be a good explanation. Maybe Mr. Fetzler just took a walk. He was worried about his wife that night. I'll talk to him. If it turns out there's anything fishy then you'll have to tell the deputies. I'll let you know. Okay?"

"I don't want my dad to be mad at me."

"I know. But, Anthony, you did the right thing in telling me. You should be proud of yourself for being honest and owning up."

"I guess."

"Maybe you could finish my mowing for me and do the edging. I'd consider that payback for messing with my mailbox."

Anthony flashes a smile for the first time. "Okay. Thanks, Mr. Arrowby." He takes his Coke out front where we soon hear the sound of the lawn mower.

Hank pours his Coke down the sink, replacing it with a beer. It's a little early in the day to be drinking beer, if you ask me, but who am I to judge? I've noticed that when humans become stressed they often resort either to liquor or chocolate. Strange.

After Anthony has left, Hank and I walk over to Stu's, but there's no response to the doorbell.

"Yoohoo!" Crabby is at her post.

Hank acts as if he didn't hear her, but then she calls, "Hank!" and there's no more pretending. We walk reluctantly across the street.

"Yes, Mrs. Crawford?"

"Stuart Fetzler isn't home."

"Really."

"He left early this morning. Probably he wants to get away before more TV crews show up. They were here yesterday, you know. I was interviewed." Crabby puffs herself up, a rooster fluffing its feathers. She may crow at any minute. "I think it's just terrible the way Stuart is being treated by the press. Talking as if he were a suspect. It's not right."

My nose tells me that a mole was near the flowerbed by the front porch last night, so I sniff more closely at its scent.

"What is that dog doing? He should be on a leash when he's out of his yard, you know."

"You're the one who called us over from our yard." The irritation in Hank's voice is palpable.

"Don't get uppity with me, Hank Arrowby. There's a law about loose dogs."

"Then I'll just take my loose dog home. Heel," Hank says to me, turning away from Crabby and marching down the sidewalk.

Just to show Crabby up, I heel perfectly beside Hank. I'm the epitome of dog obedience.

"And keep him away from that rose bush!"

Since the weather is cooler today, Hank takes me for a walk even though it's late in the morning. He seems distracted, not paying attention to my needs to sniff, and just pulls me along when I stop for an interesting odor. The only break comes when we encounter Li-Li and her owner, Mr, Scruggs. Li-Li and I sniff each other front and rear at first, then Li-Li assumes the play position, front paws down and forward, rear end high. I leap at her, only to be hauled back by Hank, who seems to have no patience today. He talks only briefly with Mr. Scruggs before turning back toward home.

As we approach our house, Brick shuffles toward us from around the corner of the Fetzler's, head down, clutching something in both hands. When he sees us, he quickly switches his hands to his back. He makes like he's going to go around us, but Hank steps to the side, blocking his way.

"Whatcha got there, Brick?" asks Hank.

"None of your business. Get out of my way."

"Since you're obviously hiding something, you've aroused my curiosity. What is it? Something for your pictures?"

Hank is speaking in a friendly tone, but I know he's dying to grab the thing, whatever it is.

Brick edges past Hank, facing toward Hank all the time. His square face is hard and expressionless, like a concrete block. "It's mine," he says. "You can't have it." Quicker than you would expect from such a solid man, he pivots away, transferring his object to the front, and scuffs the rest of the way to his house.

Hank stands still, watching. "It could be anything," he mutters to himself. "Could be something else of Sarah's, could be a piece of junk he found on Branham Lane. Anything."

It is 5:00 when Hank chances to see Stu Fetzler drive into his garage. Giving Stu time to get a little settled, we walk over to the house and Hank rings the bell. Stu has installed a peep-through in his door since the last time we were there and I'm aware that he's standing on the other side.

"I'm reduced to spying on my visitors," he says, opening the door.

"Don't blame you," says Hank. "Has it been bad?"

"Very." Stu's face is haggard and his eyes look as if they've sunk deeper into their sockets. "I'm being watched constantly. Plus that reporter keeps sniffing around like a damn dog."

I don't appreciate the analogy.

Stu doesn't offer us a seat like he usually does, resulting in our standing stiffly in the entryway.

"What's up?" Stu says.

"This is a little awkward, Stu," says Hank. "I was told something and I have to check it out."

"What do you mean?"

"You were seen at 1:00 in the morning on the night Sarah disappeared. Somebody saw you walking down Branham and through your side gate."

"What somebody?" Stu's face looks remarkably like Brick's—stony, cold, without expression.

"I can't tell you. All I can say is that I believe the person without question."

I begin to think that Stu will be rooted to the spot forever, staring into Hank's face. Suddenly he turns on his heels and walks toward the kitchen. Over his shoulder he says, "I was taking a walk, okay? I was taking a walk. I couldn't sleep."

Hank follows him. "I'm sorry, Stu. I had to ask."

"No, you don't have to ask!" Stu is shouting now. He whirls around again and advances on Hank, the stony face now crumbled into rage. "It's none of your goddam business. Get the fuck out of here!"

Hank stumbles into a retreat and we hurry home. When he gets himself a glass of water, Hank's hands are shaking. He paces the floor for awhile, then grabs the telephone,

"Pete? Pick up the phone if you're there." Hank pauses, but Pete apparently is out. "Listen, I need to run something by you. About Stu Fetzler. It's important." Hank's voice shakes as much as his hands.

I'm confused. I thought Stu had a logical answer, plus Hank doesn't usually get so shaken by someone's anger. I don't understand.

CHAPTER 25

Dinner is not a pleasant affair. Hank eats little and barely speaks to me. He phones Ann, but only gets her voice mail. I wish she were here.

We take a walk after dinner and even that is less fun than usual. Hank avoids our street, bringing me instead down Branham and through unfamiliar neighborhoods. Since all the urine smells are new to me, I have to do a lot of sniffing, which slows us down considerably. By the time we return home, night has fallen.

Hank paces around the living room. "I wish Pete would call," he says. As he passes by the TV he halts. "Hey, Sammy, let's watch a movie to cheer us up." He opens the cupboard under the TV and searches through his small collection.

"*Godfather?*" he mutters. "I don't think so. *The Hunt for Red October*! No. Ah, *Tootsie*. An oldie but goodie. Hoffman is always entertaining."

He plops the DVD into place, then settles himself with the remote on the sofa, legs stretched out on the coffee table. For awhile I watch the flickering images on the screen, but I'm soon bored. Just people yakking at each other, and not an animal in sight.

I curl up in the corner, which has a cozy feel to it. The room is dark and for a moment I amuse myself watching the television light reflected in Hank's face. I soon doze off, lulled to sleep by the actors' voices.

I'm startled awake by Hank's loud exclamation. "That's it! Holy shit! Omigod, that's how he did it! Omigod!"

I look at the TV screen to see what has electrified him, but it's only Dustin Hoffman in drag.

Probably because the darkness of the room makes me even more alert to sound, I hear a tiny click in spite of the noise from the television. The dark is disorienting, so that I'm unsure of the origin of the sound. I prick up my ears.

A tiny squeak of a floor board and a faint rustling of clothing tells me it's in the foyer. Although my eyes aren't what they used to be, especially in the dark, my nose is as good as ever and when I elevate it toward the living room doorway I recognize the scent of Stu Fetzler.

Something is terribly wrong. His smell has changed. Instead of just the comfortable, professorial man-with-a-pipe odor, there is something new, unfamiliar and dangerous. My skin crawls.

This new Stuart, this person I don't know, enters the living room quietly, stealthily, without a sound. I can barely make out his shape and I know he can't see me. Transfixed as I am in astonishment and fear, I feel as if I'm made of lead, my body so weighted down that I am unable to move.

Stu slowly and silently approaches the sofa, his body in a crouch. Hank finally spots him in his peripheral vision and struggles to raise himself from the soft cushions. Meanwhile, as if an unseen hand has flipped a switch, I suddenly am freed from my inertia and I sneak up behind Stu. Just as he lunges at Hank I sink my teeth into his leg. I get a mouthful of trouser instead of skin, but it's enough to interrupt his forward thrust, allowing Hank time to upright himself.

"What the?" The rest of Hank's sentence is a grunt, as Stu throws his body onto him, forcing him to the floor.

Something in Stu's right hand glints in the reflection from the TV and drops to the floor with a clang. Hank must have kneed him in the stomach or the groin, because Stu howls like an animal. The two of them go at it— yelling, grunting, wrestling—partly on the floor and partly upright. At one point they almost fall into the fireplace.

Hank is strong, stronger than he looks, but his gimpy leg interferes with his balance. Stu reaches toward the fireplace, hand flailing, and finds the poker. With a power that astonishes my own self, I leap into the air, driving my teeth deep into his right arm. This time it's bare skin and I pull off a hunk. Stu screams in pain. He drops the poker, but grabs it again.

At the same time, the front door bangs open, the blinding light is switched on, and Pete, still in uniform, is framed in the living room doorway. With legs braced, knees bent, and arms straight out in front of him, he points his automatic directly at Stu.

"Drop it!" he yells.

Stu releases the poker and clutches his wound with his left hand. Blood oozes out between his fingers.

"On the floor, face down, feet apart, arms above your head" barks Pete.

After Stu complies, Pete grabs Stu's arms, one at a time, positioning them behind his back, and then he handcuffs him. As Pete calls for backup on his cell phone, Stu begins to moan.

"I killed her." He chokes out the words. "Dear God, I killed Sarah. She found out. My affair with Vera. She..."

"Stu!" Pete is leaning over him now. "You have the right to remain silent. Anything you say can and will be used against you."

Stu's words override Pete's. "She was—going to tell—ruin everything I've worked for—everything ruined." Stu's breath comes in gasps.

"Do you understand? You have the right to speak to an attorney and to have an attorney..."

"Yes, yes, yes. I know."

"Present during any questioning."

Pete seems to be going through some sort of ritual and Stu doesn't want to listen.

"I don't care about that." Stu is shouting and sobbing at the same time. "You have a gun. Just shoot me. Shoot me."

He twists to look at Hank and the tears are pouring down his contorted face. "So long ago. I was an actor in New York. A girl. It wasn't rape. I thought she was my age." He sobs and spits out the words in-between gasps. "My prison record—Sarah threatened to tell everyone—ruin my project— ruin me—my life ruined." He lays his sweating head back onto the floor. "Shoot me."

Hank, who has stumbled to his feet, stares at Stu, his mouth agape and disbelief in his eyes. He starts to say something, but turns away, shaking his head.

Pete directs his attention to Hank. "Are you okay?"

Hank nods, but I see that his legs are trembling. Abruptly, he sits down on the sofa in the same spot where, what seems like an eternity ago, he simply had been watching an entertaining movie.

"Why was he attacking you?" asks Pete.

"He must have thought I knew more than I did. I didn't really figure it out until later, but by that time he was already here." Hank stares at Pete and his voice becomes a whisper. "He was going to kill me, Pete."

At the sound of sirens, Pete says, "Stuart, I'm arresting you for assault with a deadly weapon."

In response to the look of surprise on Hank's face, he says, "It's all I can do legally now. Don't worry. They'll get him on a murder charge."

Stu begins to babble incoherently, and the entrance of two San Jose officers into the room sets him off on a verbal rampage. When they haul him to his feet he yells and swears and tries to wrest away from their hold on him. This disheveled, sweating, purple-faced man can't be the same person I've known and liked for so many years.

The cops yell right back at him and there is so much commotion that I cower in the corner. It is more than I can bear. I hunker down, shivering, with my tail between my legs.

Hank finds me in the corner when it is all over and the last of them is gone. He lifts me up and carries me to the sofa, where I am never allowed. There he holds me partially in his lap, strokes me with trembling hands, and tells me what a good dog I am.

"You saved my life, Sam." His voice breaks. "This can't be real. I've known Stu Fetzler for ten years. He's my friend."

I wriggle a little in his arms and he strokes my shoulder, his fingers passing over my fur in rhythm with his words.

"He and Sarah were such a great couple. No matter what the secrets or how bad things were, he didn't have to kill her. How could he do such a thing? And he was going to kill me, too. He must be insane." His voice cracks again.

When I lift my head to lick his face, I taste salty water on his cheek.

It is the next morning and nothing seems real. The world looks different, somehow, as if we're all in a dream. Even Mrs. Crawford's behavior is unusual; she actually leaves her command post across the street this morning to knock on Hank's door, wanting to discuss the events of last night.

"I was wondering why the police were at your house last night," she says, "and then I saw on TV just now that Stuart Fetzler was arrested. They said he attacked you. Is that true?"

"Yes."

"What did he do, actually?"

"It was on the TV."

"Well, I thought you might have more to add about what happened."

"No."

Caught off guard by Hank's obvious reluctance to discuss the matter, Crabby sputters. "You know, I never did trust Stuart Fetzler. He always acted so full of himself, so sure he was always right. I'm not at all surprised that he did it."

This from the woman who was so sure about her identification of Sarah as the driver of the car. I'm the one who's surprised—that Hank doesn't laugh right in her face. Instead, he slowly starts to close the door.

"I'm sorry, Mrs. Crawford, but I don't feel like talking about it at the moment."

"Well, if you do, just come over and we'll chat." She glances in my direction. "But you can leave the animal at home."

Half an hour later the doorbell rings, and Hank mutters, "What now?" as he walks toward the door. On the doorstep is Dan O'Keefe, the reporter.

"Good morning, Mr. Arrowby," he says. He has a look of concern plastered on his face, but I think it's fake. I swear his nose is twitching in anticipation of getting all the juicy details. "May I come in?"

"No!" Hank slams the door shut. He stands there for a moment, both hands against the door and his head hanging between his arms. "No, no, no, no." The words change to sobs.

I'm so startled by his sudden loss of composure that I'm frozen in place. I watch as he turns and staggers to the nearest chair, where he sits hunched over with his hands covering his face. He continues to sob; then he lifts his face, red and drenched with tears, throws his head back and howls. It is a primitive sound that pierces my soul. I lift my head and I yowl, too.

"Sammy," he croaks, "aw, Sammy." In an instant he is on the floor beside me. He folds me into his arms and we remain that way for a long time.

CHAPTER 26

The ensuing days are hectic, what with the phone ringing constantly, more reporters bugging Hank, and neighbors dropping in uninvited. Ann has been in and out, cooking for Hank and fussing over him. It is at her suggestion that Hank invites Pete and Miriam to join them late Saturday afternoon for drinks and discussion.

On Saturday, Ann is the first to arrive. I make a beeline for her, eager for her attention, but Hank beats me to it. It gripes me that she kisses him before patting me.

Miriam and Pete walk in at almost the same time.

"Door's still unlocked, I see," says Pete. "Didn't you learn anything?"

Hank's voice is edgy. "It's daylight and I was expecting company, all right?" I think Hank is not yet recovered from last week's trauma.

With drinks poured and finger food laid out, everyone gathers around the table on the patio. I lie at Hank's feet, within easy grasp of any tidbits that might fall over the side.

"I don't get it, "says Hank. "Stu kept confessing to the murder although Pete told him his rights, and even from the jail he yakked to a reporter. His lawyer must have been having a hemorrhage."

"He probably wants to die," says Miriam.

"And murder one is one way to do it," Pete adds.

"I was surprised," says Ann. "How can he get a fair trial after all that stuff in the paper? Admitting, like he did, that he was having an affair with Vera what's-her-name and that he killed Sarah because she was going to spill the beans about his past. Tell me again: what was it he did in New York?"

"It happened when he was an actor in New York City," says Pete. "He went there right from high school, didn't go to college until after he had tried to make it in the theater. I believe he was around twenty-two when he dated this girl and had sex with her. Turned out she was only fifteen years old, although she looked much older."

"So he was charged with statutory rape."

"Right. Went to prison, but I don't think it was for very long. Then he came west, got a couple of degrees, and became a community college teacher. Nobody around here knew about his past, except Sarah, of course. Apparently, she never told her parents."

Ann shakes her head. "I don't see how he could get hired at the college if he had a criminal record."

Pete says, "At the college level I don't think they investigate potential hires for felony convictions. They're more interested in verifying whether the person actually does hold the degree he claims and whether his job history checks out."

"So he murdered Sarah," says Miriam, "because she discovered his affair with Vera Escobar and she threatened to disclose his past?"

"Apparently."

"That doesn't seem like a big enough reason to murder someone," says Ann.

Hank, chewing on a pretzel, points the broken part at Ann. "You don't understand. Stu's theater project wasn't just an important goal; it was the biggest thing in his life. It was all wound up in his ego and his very soul. If Sarah had blabbed about his criminal record, not only would this have probably ended his affair with Vera, but it also would have killed the project and in his mind that would have killed him."

"So he does the killing, instead. Very logical," says Ann, disgust written on her face.

"Have you heard anything about Brick?" Hank asks Pete. "How did he get that brooch?"

"Who knows? He claims he found it in the Fetzler's driveway. I heard he has a ton of stuff which the detectives combed through, and I think they were suspicious about some of it—you know, possible stolen goods—but couldn't prove anything."

Stolen goods? I remember the conversation between Brick and Matchstick about something they buried. Too bad I can't talk.

Miriam is eager to hear the details about Stu's attack on Hank, so Pete and Hank recount the story. Hank becomes so animated while describing the assault that he sloshes some of his beer, drops of it falling onto my nose. I lick it and hope he'll get excited again.

"I don't quite understand," says Miriam. "How did you know Stuart killed Sarah? And how did he know that you knew?"

"I didn't know for sure. I got uneasy when I found out that late at night when Sarah disappeared he was seen entering his yard from the Branham Lane side. As far as I could recall, he originally had told me that he went to sleep after waiting up late for her."

"Probably walked back home after leaving the car at Lexington Reservoir," says Pete. "He would have taken the trail from the dam, walked through Los Gatos, and then on to this area. It's a long way, but doable. Might take a couple hours."

"Who saw him that night?" asks Miriam.

"A neighborhood kid who had just finished vandalizing my mailbox. He kept quiet about it because he didn't want to get in trouble, but when he was watching TV and hearing more about Stu, he decided to tell me. I felt there must be some explanation, and I told him I'd try to find out."

"Who's the kid?" asks Pete.

"Nobody you know. Unfortunately for him, it's all going to come out now."

"So then what did you do?" Miriam asks.

"When Stu finally got home I told him about being seen. There was a moment, just a moment, when he didn't say anything, but gave me a look. I can't describe it." Hank pauses to reach for the pretzels. "You know how it is? When you look at somebody's eyes? And you can almost see the wheels going around inside their head while they're thinking of what to say? Then he turns around and starts acting all defensive, telling me he had gone out for a walk because he couldn't sleep. I still thought that could have been true, but for the first time I doubted his innocence. And he must have known. He must have thought I knew more than I did."

"So he decided to take care of you," says Pete.

"Except that you got my message and came over, thank God."

"Yes," says Pete, "there was something about the tone of your voice, an urgency. The house was dark when I arrived, but I heard the noise inside. The rest everybody knows. Except there was nothing in the paper about your dog biting the hell out of Stuart. Where is Sammy, anyway?"

"He's near me, under the table," says Ann.

"Give that dog a pretzel. And some beer," says Pete.

Everyone laughs when Pete tosses me a pretzel and Hank pours a little of his drink into my open mouth. I should be a hero more often.

"The odd thing is," says Hank, "I didn't really know Stu had done it until I was watching a DVD of *Tootsie* and it was at that precise moment that he decided to come after me."

"*Tootsie?*" says Miriam. "You mean that old movie? I don't get it."

Hank explains. "Dustin Hoffman plays an out-of-work actor who disguises himself as a woman in order to get a role that happens to be female. When I saw him in that getup it suddenly hit me. It was Stu, not Sarah, whom Crabby saw driving away. All he needed to do was wear a blonde wig, a white shirt, and Sarah's floppy hat. He's a former actor and a drama teacher, remember? It was a no-brainer for him."

"The paper said she was probably killed at home," says Miriam. "That means her body was in the car when he drove away. The thought of it makes me sick."

"They still don't know the murder weapon," says Pete. "The autopsy only showed that it was a blunt object."

Hank suddenly sits bolt upright with a look of surprise on his face. "I know what it was! Their mortar and pestle was missing when I went to borrow it. Stu claimed not to even know what I was talking about. That sonofabitch!" Hank bangs his fist on the table and everyone's glass bounces. "What gets me is that this man was my friend. A nice guy. Someone I really liked. I can't get it through my head that he's a murderer."

"Happens all the time," says Pete, "Appearances are deceiving. You think you know someone, but you really don't. And when the case is extreme, like this one, it really messes with your head."

Miriam nods vehemently. "Which is why talking about the experience is so important. Thank you, Hank, for setting up this little get-together."

"Don't thank me," says Hank. "Thank Annie. It was her idea."

Miriam swirls the straw in her lemonade. I find it interesting that she is the only one not drinking beer or wine. "I suppose," she says, "that it's the therapist in me coming to the fore here, but I do believe it would be helpful for us to talk about our feelings. After such a traumatic event we need to be in touch with what's really happening inside us and not feel that we must be strong and carry on as usual. Everyone has a lot of processing to do. And that includes me." She takes a long pull on her straw.

The others suddenly take an interest in their drinks, avoiding Miriam's gaze.

"It might help if I start," Miriam says. "My most immediate feeling is one of anger: anger at Stuart for killing my wonderful partner; anger with myself for not trying harder to understand why Sarah seemed so preoccupied those last days; anger with the media for behaving like vultures." She shakes her head. "And then I feel so terribly sad. Just plain sad."

Miriam sighs and looks at Ann. "Ann, you are the most removed from the situation, but it must have affected you, too."

Ann frowns and there is a pause before she answers. "I never knew Sarah and only met Stu a couple of times, but I have seen what this mess has done to Hank. I guess you'd say my biggest feeling is worry about him. That's the main thing. Worry."

Miriam tries to get her to elaborate, but Ann clams up. I get the feeling she is fighting back tears. Miriam-the-Therapist, I'm sure, would be happier if Ann would just let go. Knowing Ann as I do, I think there will be plenty of tears later on when she is alone with Hank.

"How about you, Pete?"

Pete rolls his tongue inside his cheek and looks up at the tree, maybe expecting the answer to drift down to him. I don't think cops like to discuss feelings. "Relief," he says. "I feel relieved. From the get-go I figured Stu was the perp and I'm positive the deputies thought so, too, especially since they would have discovered early on that he had a record. So I was frustrated that it was taking so long for them to get enough evidence to charge him. And like you, Ann, I was worried about Hank. All his sniffing around was asking for trouble." He grins at Hank. "So I'm relieved that my friend, Sherlock Holmes, is alive and well."

Everyone looks at Hank. "It's hard," he says. "Hard to sort out all the feelings I have. Grief. Lots of grief. Feeling betrayed. Depressed. Mostly, though, I'm angry. Very, very angry. Sarah was a beautiful, loving, generous woman and he took her life away, just like that."

I'm angry, too. I'm angry at Stu. I'm angry that people aren't always as they seem. I'm angry that Mrs. Crawford is a busybody and she got it all wrong from the start, throwing suspicion away from Stu. Plus she is nasty to me.

I notice that the gate to the yard is ajar. While everyone remains engrossed in the discussion, I sneak out to the front yard and cross the street. Crabby Crawford is sitting in her usual spot on her front porch. When she spots me she stands up and opens her mouth, ready to spew abusiveness at me.

I look her straight in the eye, lift my leg, and pee all over her damn rose bush.

ACKNOWLEDGEMENTS

My deep appreciation goes to the following people: Chuck McCoy, for his enthusiastic role as "tech adviser"; Dean Baker, for educating me in the Interview Room at the Sheriff's Department; Liesel Ernst, for explaining the job of firefighter; Adair Lara, for her invaluable editing; John Eichinger, for his computer skills when disaster hit the manuscript; Jill Kroh, for her cheerleading efforts; Juli Cortino, Kathy Leong, and Shelly Monfort for their honest critiques, unwavering support, and cherished friendship.

I am extremely grateful to them all.